PLAUTUS IN THE CONVENT

THE MONK'S MARRIAGE

Conrad Ferdinand Meyer

PLAUTUS
IN THE CONVENT

•

THE
MONK'S MARRIAGE

Two Novellas

With an introduction by
KONRAD SCHAUM
Princeton University

FREDERICK UNGAR PUBLISHING CO.
NEW YORK

Translated by William Guild Howard from
PLAUTUS IM NONNENKLOSTER *and* DIE HOCHZEIT DES MÖNCHES

Printed in the United States of America

Library of Congress Catalog Card No. 64-20048

INTRODUCTION

The course of Meyer's life was—as the poet himself phrased it—"actually unbelievably strange"; it combined great contrasts: extreme immobility and intense activity, uninspired aimlessless and continuous inner growth, paralyzing inhibitions and poetic accomplishments: unique strength and purity of form. The enigma of his own psychological evolution often became a source of depressive contemplation in his youth and early manhood. Born in 1825, the eldest son of a distinguished patrician family in Zürich, the young Meyer seemed to find no appropriate function within society. Far into his thirties he lived like an invalid excluded from every normal relationship, isolated from his surroundings by his oversensitivity and apparent lack of bourgeois determination. The early death of his father, a privy councillor, left him in the care of his mother who, despite certain similarities of character, scarcely understood her introverted and unambitious son. She herself suffered from extreme loneliness and was obsessed by prejudiced and sentimental piety. Meyer's younger sister, Betsy, a person of tender and self-sacrificing devotion, was closer to him but could not help him find a form of life adequate to his inner impulses and expectations.

During these years of isolation and suffering, Meyer tried his hand at poetry and painting; he also studied history and literature but these attempts were unsystematic and lacked perseverance. It would be unjust, however, to view these years of searching as a period of emptiness and lack of accomplishment. Throughout his life, Meyer was an avid reader, and it seemed that his particular talent could develop only through a long period of growth. His intellectual attitude was that of "internalization," of an impressionistic acceptance of the surrounding world in its fullest orchestration, from which he abstracted its most characteristic law and "reality." He came to respect life in its most significant and vital forms but he remained at a contemplative distance and in an indirect relationship to the things around him in order to construct a "third reality" between himself and the world: the carefully balanced harmony of his poetic imagery.

In spite of his passionate yearning to liberate himself from his narrow bourgeois environment and from an atmosphere of social and spiritual prejudice and rigidity, to break through his "monastic isolation," Meyer was more dedicated than rebellious. His goal could not be a simple and immediate participation in life; his fulfillment was in life's elemental and most universal forces and principles within the realm of art. Keeping in mind that his synthesizing imagery combines a vast multiplicity of important traits and forces, one will understand in how difficult a way his sensitive impressionism developed. In essence, Meyer spent the long period of his maturity as a restless wanderer through various philosophical, artistic, historical, and geographical phases of human evolution in search of what he considered the foundations of human existence, the "natural laws" fundamental to all forms of human life.

The intense psychological crisis which befell Meyer in 1852 may in part have grown out of the increasing richness and depth of his perceptive mind. The more powerful his inner vision of life's drama, the more depressing he must have felt the lack of creative expression. Increasing neurotic symptoms led to a brief stay in an asylum in Préfargier near Neuchâtel. This short crisis, however, was the transition to a more productive period which began with the influence of Mr. Vulliemin and his family, whose guest he was for several months after his release from Préfargier. This old friend of his father's helped him to receive a contract to translate Thierry's *Récits des temps Mérovingiens*. This new activity, which continued after his return to Zürich, became a valuable exercise in style and brought about an enrichment of his historical knowledge; but during the subsequent years the old atmosphere provided little stimulation to further some of his new poetic concepts.

A more marked change in his life was brought about by the mental illness of his mother, who was taken to Préfargier where she took her life in a state of total depression and remorse. She wrote of her son shortly before her death: "In spite or rather because of my motherly tenderness, I am the person who is most detrimental for him."

In the following year Meyer began to travel, first to Paris, then to Munich, Rome, and later to Venice. An inheritance from a relative made him financially independent. His plan to study law was soon abandoned; he turned instead to extensive literary studies, especially of French authors, and soon displayed greater confidence and skill as a lyric poet. Visiting many galleries, he developed an unusual receptivity to the creative arts, and it is significant that his actual realm of intellectual experience came not through the immediate relationship between himself and nature but through the medium of art. Meyer carefully avoids two extremes: for him art was neither an abstracted reproduction of nature nor an exaggerated expression of his own ego. The artistic form in his view is to a high degree based on symbolic effects created by confronting the infinite possibilities of the world with the equally varied sphere of man's soul. Meyer's style originates in a process of slow assimilation and mutual balance of inner and outer forces, culminating in a subtle fusion of nature and soul. "I actually work without interruption," he admitted to a friend, "but very slowly, and I truly cultivate this phlegmatic habit because I recognize my security in this precious natural tendency."

Meyer was almost forty-six years of age when his cycle of poems, *Hutten's Last Days*, became his first literary success. With the year 1871 a period of rich and fruitful literary creativity began and lasted nearly two decades. Almost simultaneously he worked on his epic *Enyelberg*, his longest prose work *Jürg Jenatsch*, and his novella *Das Amulett*. During the first years of his productivity his sister Betsy helped him as a faithful companion. In 1875 he married the young Luise Ziegler, who gave him a long desired happiness and drew him closer to society. Other works followed in constant succession: *Der Schuss von der Kanzel* (1877), *Der Heilige* (1878), *Plautus im Nonnenkloster* (1881), *Gedichte* (1882), *Gustav Adolphs Page* (1882), *Das Leiden eines Knaben* (1883), *Die Hochzeit des Mönches* (1883/84), *Die Richterin* (1885), *Die Versuchung des Pescara* (1887). After a brief illness he completed his last novella, *Angela Borgia* (1891), but could not finish a longer historical novel, *Der Dynast*, and other planned works. He suffered a complete nervous breakdown and remained during the last years before his death in 1898 in a state of inactive melancholy.

Plautus in the Convent (1881) may appear at first glance to be a humorous and ironic Renaissance study, the remarkable plot of which is elaborately supplemented with a wealth of humanistic details and interesting perspectives. Meyer, however, warned that we not be deceived by the "comical mask" and not overlook the "serious foundation of the little novella." The gravity within the free play of poetic composition lies in the fact that the three protagonists embody, according to Meyer's own interpretation, "the three historical conditions of the Reformation . . . : the secularization of the higher clergy (Poggio the true prototype of a humanist: witty intellectualism, frivolity, silly imitation and overestimation of antiquity, insincerity, vindictiveness . . . larceny and mendicancy . . .)." There is further the human deterioration of the lower clergy, represented by the abbess Brigitte whose "crude falsehood contrasts with the more refined one of Poggio," and both of them are in opposition to Gertrude, who symbolizes "the honest foundation of the common people's nature without which the Reformation would have been an impossibility."

It is obvious that this simple key immediately illuminates certain details of motivation, but it does not explain the narrative as a whole. The entire phenomenon of Reformation is transformed and reflected upon a uniquely personal plane where the inner psychological implications of such a metamorphosis of life are determining factors. Meyer does not represent an actual event of history but a fundamental and timeless act of inner liberation and rebirth. In Meyer's ironic craft of fiction the historical phenomenon merely reflects an original and essentially unchangeable order of existence.

Thus we realize that knowledge of the Reformation is not a prerequisite for a better understanding of the novella in its most significant features. We must be convinced, however, of the truth and effectiveness of the spiritual and psychic forces which Meyer intended to bring to life in the three protagonists and in their relationship to each other. The typical forms of mental activity and destiny, as they are given here, are not confined to the actual conditions of the sixteenth century but are perhaps more applicable to the intellectual situation of Meyer's own time, in which the birth of a "new man" was so intensely desired.

In this view the portrait of Poggio takes on another dimension: We see the extreme flexibility and playful dominance of the rational mind but also a conspicuous lack of ethical instinct. This enthusiastic aesthete indistinguishably combines greatness and baseness, amiability and deceit, creativity and destructiveness. In spite of selfish fraudulence he represents high intellectual talents; he is a "highwayman" and yet gifted with a vivid sense of beauty. His function is to unmask a false form of religion but he is unable to set forth any conviction of his own. Such learned epicurism and vagrant aesthetic ecclecticism far transcend any intended portrait of the typical humanist; the picture seems rather to come much closer to the instinctless intellectualism and historicism of modern civilization which Nietzsche so severely criticized.

Similarly, the abbess Brigitte must be seen not only as an example of a "dehumanized clergy" but also as "skillful administrator" inspired by a resolute and ambitious business spirit depicted by Meyer not without a touch of ironic respect, although its dubious consequences are only too obvious. The militant and unscrupulously deceitful abbess is also viewed as the product of her social and institutionalized environment, which again throws light upon "eternally recurring" attitudes of human life.

Gertrude in her straightforward honesty is certainly the most sympathetic figure in the novella but she is by no means idealized. In Meyer's "realistic" aspect the destiny of simple humanity and goodness is filled with suffering and affliction. Gertrude's dilemma is not only the liberation from an unnatural bond but also the overcoming of an inherent dichotomy of life. Her solemn vow to enter the convent if her mother were spared an untimely death is just as real within her heart as her love for Hans. In her world, which cannot exist "without faith and trust," she has to overcome the discrepancy between reason and feeling in order to gain "relief of the heart." This struggle, however, leads her into the very center of tragic experience. No mere protestation based on self-confident conviction is possible. Gertrude has to take up the heavy cross and gain her freedom in painful fulfillment of her vow. No rational deliberation, no change of fortune can help the soul in this reformation of life in accordance with an inner and more humane truth. The spiritual rebirth of modern man, which Meyer's art essentially symbolizes, is more than a mental decision: it takes place in the physical as well as in the psychological sphere. "Violent screams," "stupefying downfall" and grotesque outbursts of frenzy and despair are only side-effects of this forceful re-establishment of elemental inner necessities.

Meyer's poetic intentions thus culminate in the creation of characters and actions which reveal a fundamental structure of human destiny, and this at a time when binding concepts of human values as well as a feeling for ethical distinctions seemed to be destroyed by materialistic, historistic and positivistic views.

The Monk's Marriage (1883-84) is perhaps the most demanding of Meyer's narratives; its plot is structured in such an intricate and complex way that it immediately suggests an almost unlimited flux, a great multiplicity and fortuitousness in the basic conditions of man's life. A new concept of fate and super-individual determinism is reflected in a context of events that fundamentally calls into question whatever man's initiative and free will attempt to achieve. The other most characteristic feature of Meyer's style is a subtle but deep and very convincing depiction of the elemental impulses and forces of the human psyche.

Meyer uses three poetic means to reach full representation of the external as well as internal reality as he perceives it: he creates the illusion of time and history in order to bring out the determining social and political presuppositions of destiny; he is a master of poetic irony in the sense of maintaining a constant flexibility of perspective; closely related to this is Meyer's elaborate use of the traditional "frame-technique" of the novella, forcing the reader to assume a more objective, detached, and contemplative attitude. Reflecting upon this narrative device, Meyer admitted that he had chosen his technique "quite instinctively," seeking to project his subject matter "as far away from the eye as possible" in order to "shape the theme in a sovereign way." This superiority and freedom in handling his material may be considered as the author's re-action to his intense awareness of the complexity of our social, historical, and psychological possibilities. He needed distance, irony, and symbolic perspectives if he intended to penetrate and to touch the foundations of life, which he experienced, similarly to Nietzsche and other contemporaries, as being dy-namically changing and relative.

Before the story of the unfrocked monk is developed from a nucleus of popular fables and proverbs, Meyer skillfully un-folds a "frame-action" in which the old and exiled Dante ap-pears as the narrator at the court of Cangrande in fourteenth-century Verona. The central story or "inner plot" serves as a kind of pastime entertainment for the court, which bears all the earmarks of a truly "modern" society. In a deliberately artistic but carefully balanced fashion, the stage is set to guide our imagination into more elementary stratas of human life and to re-examine basic principles of our moral and social existence. The historical motivation is merely a part of the ironic struc-ture of Meyer's fiction, which is totally directed toward achiev-ing more objective and unprejudiced insight into fnudamental human problems. Only in this context can the wider implica-tions and general significance of the moral problem indicated in the external motivation of the story be properly recognized. Because it is not the repeated breach of sacred vows that inter-ested the poet but the shaping of a true and important human fate by intertwining two equally strong and justifiable reali-ties with one another: that of man's inner forces and that of any given social order. The actual theme of the story is life's eternal, tragic juxtaposition of reason and feeling, of mind and heart, of body and spirit. The particular form in which this duality of life appears in this story is that of justice and mercy.

Justice is represented by Ezzelino, who seeks to preserve unity and order with the iron fist of a tyrant; but justice is also the principle of all communal life and motivates in a most extreme form the cunning cleverness of the monk's father, which forces Astorre to break his solemn vow and to promise his hand to his brother's widow for the sake of continuing the family. Under the aspect of justice, the "continuation of the family is praised as God's highest blessing." Even the powerful ruler Ezzelino cannot destroy this original demand of justice and prevent the dying Vicedomini from defeating his son with his own weapon by challenging his compassion and charity through gambling with the salvation of his soul in the face of death. But the unique and incomparable event of this story is not the compelled "change of profession," the unwilling involvement of the monk in worldly life, but rather the unfolding of the inmost principle of his soul in the midst of external life as the realm of justice. Astorre changes the form of his life but not the predominant law of his spiritual existence. It becomes his destiny, as his friend ironically remarks, "to carry mercy into a world in which simple goodness scarcely remains unpunished."

Meyer fully preserves the equilibrium of both forces. Astorre is neither a rebel against the institution of the church nor is he drawn into life by any temptation. He was a good monk actively and unselfishly dedicated to his sacred office of charity. He completely fulfilled his function within the total order of things representing highest spiritual values of man. "May the monks die out," Dante emphatically states, "as soon as a human generation arises which is capable of uniting the two highest forces of the human soul which seem to exclude one another, namely, justice and mercy." The very principle of his being caused him to yield to his father's will. Yet, it is equally true that this highest sacrifice exposes him now to unknown dangers which ultimately must destroy his individual life. He is not tempted by an "awakened worldly desire or worldly vigour" nor has he misjudged his nature; but he "becomes unfaithful to himself, be it out of sacred reasons of piety, and he breaks a vow which he had made to himself more than to the church and casts off a cowl which fits his body and does not burden him." The unavoidable tragedy implied in these words is the continuous disintegration of the individual personality, culminating in the sacrifice of the self in love. If Astorre is forced to realize mercy within a world "which follows its own laws," the abandonment of his own "bright star" of destiny and an entirely new way of fulfillment appear to be necessary.

In the ensuing struggle between the "two highest forces of the human soul," we observe that the given concepts of good and evil grow conspicuously relative and vague. Astorre breaks his public betrothal with Diana and enters into an adventurous marriage with Antiope; he disregards all established codes of society and even defies the basic laws of justice.

From Astorre's viewpoint, however, the same chain of events looks entirely different: he was willing to keep his promise but is also compelled to respond to the situation according to the dictates of his soul. Only the external postulations have changed, not his inner standards and principles. Pure chance and an arbitrary play of possibilities involve him with Antiope, but once he had rediscovered in her the image of highest beauty and goodness which had long been dormant in his mind, a new and stronger reality develops and dominates all of his actions. Meyer creates an almost miraculous kinship of souls—Astorre had already felt an intense feeling for Antiope when he witnessed her attempt to share her father's execution. He is again seized by compassion and love when she sacrifices herself for her mother. No concept of guilt can arise from these actions— "the monk could not be touched by vulgarity. A creative fire drove from Antiope's hand into his own . . ." Love becomes the new realm of life in which the principle of mercy assumes an exclusive rulership. Common morality, duty, honor, and peace are of secondary importance.

In contrast to the order of the world which Ascanio calls a mixture of "seriousness and play, virtue and lust, faithfulness and inconstancy, good faith and clever mistrust," the order of creative love generates a dreamlike unity of feeling, a miraculous redemption from all mundane duality. While the rigorous spirit of justice gives life its necessary form and limitation, the bestowing of mercy is a divine gift which demands absolute submission. Only Astorre in his seeming weakness and unworldliness can be the perfect champion of man's highest force of creation. The creative power of love in its absolute form, however, does not only contradict and transcend the common form of temporal existence, it also enters into a tragic paradox: Astorre cannot separate his complete dedication and love from the given conditions of earthly life; he must bear the full tension between the spiritual and the material.

The ultimate victory of mercy and love in time is sacrifice, abandonment of every individual and singular form of life. But the experience of tragedy in Meyer's perspective is not defeat or the result of guilt; it rather indicates the most intensive realization of our human forces. The fatal exclusion of two fundamental elements of our inner impulses from one another is nothing but a possibility of our earthly reality; genuine tragedy always contains a fruitful and creative perspective which Meyer projects in the direction of a simple and unconditional submission to the universal principle. Both justice and mercy, reason and feeling, will and love, are only seeming disparities, and whenever they are completely separated, tragic destruction indirectly reflects their necessary relativity. This cannot be complete unity but an organic and creative polarity which is actually anchored in the basic impulses of man himself. Thus the delineation of Astorre's fate is to convey a complete image of all essential forces and conditions which determine man's destiny; it is also intended to deepen our understanding of the elemental forces of man's soul, whose role in winning a new human dimension of reality Meyer clearly perceived and symbolically represented.

K. S.

PLAUTUS IN THE CONVENT

O enjoy the cool of evening after a hot summer day a company of cultivated Florentines had assembled, in front of a pavilion in the Medici gardens, about Cosimo de' Medici, the "father of his country." The dusk crept by slow degrees over a gorgeous but delicately shaded, cloudless sky above the group of temperate revelers, in which a sharp-featured, gray-haired man was conspicuous, whose eloquent lips held the listening circle spellbound. The expression of his animated countenance was a strange mixture: over the serene brow and the smiling corners of the mouth lay the shadow of a sad experience.

When a pause ensued, Cosimo, with the shrewd eyes in an ill-favored face, spoke out and said, " Poggio, my friend, I have lately been browsing again in the little volume of your *Facetiæ*. To be sure, I know it by heart, and this I could not but regret, since I was now able to take pleasure only in the happy turns of a supple style, without the former sensation either of curiosity or of surprise. Fastidious as you are, it is impossible that you should not have excluded from the authorized edition of the book one or another of your droll and amiable pleasantries, whether because it was too spicy, or because it was not spicy enough. Try to recollect. Favor these friends, who will understand the most veiled allusion and excuse the boldest jest, with a *Facetia inedita*. Telling your story and sipping your wine " — he pointed to the goblet — " you will forget your sorrow."

---

* Permission H. Haessel, Leipzig.

The fresh grief to which Cosimo alluded, as to a matter of common report about town, had befallen the venerable Poggio — present secretary of the Florentine Republic, past secretary to five popes, formerly a cleric and latterly a family man — at the hands of one of his sons, of whom all were brilliantly endowed and all worthless. This miscreant had disgraced the gray hairs of his father by an act which came close to theft and robbery, and which, moreover, imposed upon the thrifty Poggio, his bondsman, a serious financial sacrifice.

After a little reflection the old man replied, " Those and similar pleasantries which are to your liking, friend Cosimo, comport, like flowery wreaths, only with brown locks, and sound ill from the lips of a toothless graybeard.'' Smiling, he displayed a fine row of white teeth. "And,'' he sighed, " only with reluctance do I return to these youthful frivolities, harmless as in themselves they may be, now that I behold my open-mindedness and my easy-going philosophy of life degenerate in my son — I know not by what uncanny law of increase — into intolerable impudence, even into profligacy.''

" Poggio, you are preaching!'' interposed a youth. " You, who have given back to the world the comedies of Plautus!''

" Thank you for your warning, Romolo!'' cried the unhappy father, collecting himself; for, as a good companion, he too thought it improper to burden the guests with his domestic troubles. " Thank you for reminding me. *The Discovery of Plautus* is the *Facetia* with which, indulgent friends, I will entertain you today.''

" Call it rather *The Rape of Plautus*,'' interrupted a scoffer.

But Poggio, without deigning to look at him, continued, " May it please you, friends, and at the same time demonstrate how unjust is the reproach with which the envious pursue me, that in a dishonorable, reprehensible way I have appropriated to myself those classics of which they cannot deny I am the discoverer — that, to put it bluntly, I have stolen them. Nothing is farther from the truth.''

A smile went about the circle, in which Poggio at first gravely declined to join, but in which finally he also participated; for as one who knew human nature he was aware that even the falsest prejudices can be uprooted only with difficulty.

'' My *Facetia*,'' he said, with a parody of the inclusive summary usually prefixed to an Italian short-story, '' has to do with two crosses, a heavy and a light one, and with two barbarian nuns, a novice and an abbess.''

'' Fit for the gods, Poggio,'' a neighbor interrupted him, '' like those simple-minded German vestals with whom, in your admirable letters from abroad, you peopled as with naiads the healing springs along the Limmat — by the nine muses, the best thing you have written! That letter circulated in a thousand copies all over Italy.''

'' I exaggerated, knowing your taste,'' said Poggio jocosely. ''At any rate, Ippolito, you, as a lover of simple-mindedness, will delight in my barbarian nun. And so I begin.

In those days, illustrious Cosimo, when we were lopping off the superfluous heads of our holy church, lately become a hydra, I found myself in Constance and actively devoted myself to the magnificent business of an ecumenical council. My leisure time, however, I divided between contemplation of the stimulating spectacle which had crowded upon the narrow stage of a German imperial city the piety, science, and statecraft of the century, with its popes, heretics, mountebanks, and courtesans, and the occasional search for manuscripts in the neighboring monasteries.

Following up various clues and trails, I came to the supposition, amounting to certainty, that in a nearby convent there was a Plautus in the hands of the barbarian nuns, having strayed thither as a legacy or as a pledge from some impoverished Benedictine abbey. A Plautus! Imagine, illustrious patron, what that meant at a time when our curiosity was being so unbearably goaded by the few fragments then extant of the great Roman comedian. That I could not sleep you may well believe, Cosimo — you who share and encourage my enthusiasm for the relics of a greater world which has declined and fallen. Would that I had left everything in the lurch and had hastened to the spot where an immortal, instead of delighting the world, lay moldering in ignoble obscurity! But those were the days when the election of a new pope occupied the minds of all men and the Holy Spirit was beginning to turn the attention of the assembled fathers to the merits and virtues of Otto Colonna; though this is not to say that the daily and hourly running about of his adherents and servants, of whom I was one, had thereby become any the less necessary.

Thus it happened that an inferior and dishonest searcher, unfortunately a fellow-countryman of ours, in whose presence I had, in the joy of my heart, indiscreetly mentioned the possibility of so great a discovery, anticipated me, and — blunderer that he was — instead of getting the classic by fair means or foul, aroused the suspicion of the abbess of the convent in which it lay buried in dust, and directed her attention to the treasure which she unwittingly possessed.

Finally I got a free hand and, in spite of the impending papal election, mounted a sturdy mule, leaving orders that a messenger should be dispatched to me upon the occurrence of the great event. My mule-driver was a Rhætian who had come to Constance in the retinue of the Bishop of Chur, and his name was Hans of Splügen. He had unhesitatingly accepted my first offer and we had agreed upon an incredibly low sum.

A thousand pleasantries passed through my mind. The blue ether, the summer air tempered by a cool, almost cold breath from the north, the inexpensive trip, the difficulties of the papal election happily overcome, the supreme satisfaction awaiting me in the discovery of a classic — these heavenly benefits disposed me to infinite good-humor, and I heard the muses and the angels sing. My companion, on the contrary, Hans of Splügen, abandoned himself, as it seemed, to the most melancholy reflections.

Happy myself, I benevolently sought to make him happy also, or at least to cheer him up, and I gave him all sorts of riddles — mostly from biblical history, which is familiar to the people. " Do you know," I asked, " the manner in which the prince of the apostles was freed from his chains? " And I received the answer that he had seen the miracle depicted in the church of the Apostles at Tosana. " Listen, Hänsel," I continued. " The angel said unto Peter, ' Bind on thy sandals and follow me.' And they went, Peter not knowing that it was an angel, past the first and the second ward, through the gate and along a street. And forthwith the companion departed and then Peter said, ' Now I know of a surety that an angel hath led me.' From what circumstance, Hänsel, did this sudden knowledge, this incontrovertible certainty come to him? Tell me that, if you can guess it." Hans thought a while and then shook the curly locks of his hard head. " Listen, Hänsel," I said, " I will answer the question. From this circumstance Peter recognized the angel, that he asked no gratuity for his services. Such is not the way of this world. That is the way only of the heavenly beings! "

But one ought not to jest with the people. Hänsel suspected in this joke, born of nothing, a purpose or an allusion.

" It is true, sir, that I am conducting you for almost nothing, and that, though I am not an angel, I shall ask you for no gratuity. Know, then, that I also on my own account am drawn to Monasterlingen " — he mentioned the name of the nunnery which was the goal of our expedition —" where tomorrow Gertrude will wind the rope girdle about her hips, and her blond hair will be shorn from her head."

Tears rolled down the sunburnt face of the hardy youth who, I may add,—perhaps there was a drop of Roman blood in his veins—possessed much natural dignity of speech and action. "By Cupid's bow," I exclaimed, "an unhappy lover!" and bade him tell me his story, which proved to be simple but by no means easy to understand.

Hänsel had, he said, come with his bishop to Constance, and being without employment, had sought work in the neighborhood as a carpenter. He had found it on some buildings in process of erection for the nunnery, and had made the acquaintance of Gertrude, who lived nearby. They had learned to like each other and found favor in each other's sight. Gladly and often they had sat together—"in all decency and honor," said he, "for she is a good girl." Then suddenly she had withdrawn from him, without detriment to their love, but peradventure as though a strictly limited time had elapsed; and he had heard for certain that she intended to take the veil. To-morrow she was to be invested, and he had in mind to attend this ceremony, in order to have the testimony of his own eyes to the fact that an honest and by no means impulsive girl could, for no conceivable reason, leave a man whom she confessedly loved, to become a nun—to embrace duties for which Gertrude, a natural woman and full of life, was as unsuited as she could possibly be, and for which, to judge from her own expressions, she had no desire, but rather recoiled from them with horror and dread.

"It is unexplainable," the melancholy Rhætian concluded; and added that through the mercy of heaven his wicked stepmother had recently died, on whose account he had left his father's house; so that this and the arms of his aged father were again open to receive him. His love, accordingly, would now find a warm nest awaiting her; but she was incomprehensibly determined to nestle in a cell.

At the close of this speech Hänsel relapsed into his dark brooding and obstinate silence, which he interrupted only to answer my question concerning the kind of woman the abbess was. He said she was an ugly little person, but an excellent manager who had restored and rehabilitated from slovenliness the economic administration of the convent. She came from Abbatis Cella and people called her simply "Brigittchen of Trogen."

Finally the convent appeared above the sky-line of monotonous vineyards. Hänsel now asked me to leave him behind at an inn by the roadside, since he wished to see Gertrude only once more — at her investiture. I nodded assent and dismounted from the mule, in order to stroll at leisure toward the not distant convent.

There they were having a merry time. On the lawn of the convent yard an indistinguishable great object was being sold at auction or exhibited for some other purpose. A rough soldier, with his helmet on his head, blew from time to time a discordant trumpet, perhaps a piece of booty, perhaps an ecclesiastical instrument. About the abbess, with her nuns, and the questionable herald in a patched doublet and tattered hose, whose bare toes peered forth from his worn-out boots, laity and an aggregation of monks formed a motley group in the most free and easy attitudes. Among the peasants stood here and there a nobleman — in Turgovia, as this German district is called, there is an overabundance of such small and petty crested fowl — but minstrels, gypsies, vagabonds, strumpets, and rabble of every sort, attracted thither by the Council, also mingled in the strange circle. One after another, they stepped forth and tried the weight of the object in which, upon nearer approach, I recognized a gigantic old horrible cross. It seemed to be extraordinarily heavy; for after a short while it began to sway back and forth in the wearying hands of even the strongest bearer; it threatened to fall, and would have come crashing down if other hands and shoulders had not tumultuously put themselves under the ponderous beams. Shouts and laughter accompanied the scandalous performance. To complete the ignoble scene, the boorish abbess danced about like one possessed upon the freshly mown lawn, inspired by the worth of her relic — the meaning of this country fair began to dawn upon me — and probably also inspirited by the convent wine which, without cups and without ceremony, passed in huge wooden buckets from lip to lip.

"By the tresses of the Virgin Mother!" shrieked the impious jade, "not a man of you, not even the stoutest, can lift and carry this cross of our blessed Duchess Amala-swinta; but tomorrow our Gertrude will toss it like a shuttle-cock. I only hope the mortal creature will not grow vain! To God alone the glory, says Brigittchen. People, the miracle is a thousand years old and to this day is brand new. It has always worked, and upon my word it shall go off tomorrow without a hitch." Manifestly the excellent abbess had had a drop too much in the course of this heavenly day.

Comparing these comical doings with similar events that I have witnessed in my own blessed country, I began to understand them and to estimate them at their true value — just as, an hour later, with fuller knowledge of the facts, I definitively solved the problem; but the trend of my thoughts was suddenly and unpleasantly interrupted by a shrill call of the clownish woman in the white cowl, with the flushed face, the blinking, crafty eyes, the scarcely discoverable pug-nose, and the bestial mouth gaping at an enormous distance below it.

"Hi, there, Italian scribe!" she yelled at me. I was on this day clad in a simple traveling costume and carry the evidence of my classical origin in my countenance. "Come a bit nearer and let me see you lift the cross of the blessed Amalaswinta!"

All eyes were turned in expectation of amusement at me, people made way for me, and with rude jolts in the Swiss fashion shoved me forward. I excused myself on the ground, well known to you, my friends, of the shortness and weakness of my arms.— The narrator raised his arms enough to reveal the fact.

Then the shameless woman, looking me over, cried out, " Your fingers are all the longer for it, you smooth customer! "—and in fact, by the daily practice of writing, my fingers have become developed and pliant. The crowd of bystanders burst into a boisterous laugh, incomprehensible to me, but offensive, and I charged the abbess with it. In vexation I turned away, went around the corner of the church nearby, and finding the main portal open, I entered. The noble round arch of the windows and ceiling, instead of the new-fangled pointed arch and the foolish French filigree, restored my soul to peace and composure. Slowly I strode forward the length of the nave, attracted by a piece of sculpture which, lighted from above, stood forth in impressive solidity from the religious dimness and seemed, in its way, to be a thing of beauty. I went up to it and was not disappointed. The statuary consisted of two figures united by a cross, and this cross completely resembled in size and proportions the one exhibited on the lawn, whichever may have been imitated from the other. A powerful woman crowned with thorns was carrying it almost level in brawny arms and on her mighty shoulder, and yet was sinking beneath its weight, as was shown by her knees, roughly outlined on her gown. By the side and in front of this tottering giantess a smaller figure, with a little crown upon her lovely head, mercifully placed her more delicate shoulder under the unbearable burden. The old master had purposely—or more probably from lack of artistic resources—treated the forms and garments only in the rough, reserving his cunning and the ardor of his soul for the faces, which expressed despair and mercy.

Taken with the charm of this expression, I stepped backward to get a better light. Lo and behold, there knelt before me on the other side of the group a maiden, presumably a native, a peasant girl of the vicinity, almost as powerfully built as the sculptured duchess, and with the hood of her white cowl thrown back over heavy braids of blond hair and a sturdy neck unused to concealment.

She arose; for absorbed in meditation, she had not sooner become aware of my presence than I of hers; brushed away a flood of tears from her eyes, and made a move as if to depart. She was to all appearances a novice.

I detained her and asked her to explain the statue to me. I was one of the foreign fathers at the Council, I told her in my broken German. This information did not seem to make much impression upon her. She related to me in a simple way that the image represented an ancient queen or duchess, the founder of this convent, who, taking the vow here, had wished to proceed to the investiture, her head crowned with thorns and her shoulder laden with the cross. "They say," continued the girl doubtfully, "that she was a great sinner, heavy laden with guilt for the murder of her husband, but of such high station that secular justice could not reach her. Then God touched her heart and she fell into great distress, despairing of the salvation of her soul!" After a long and bitter atonement, craving a sign that she was forgiven, she had caused this great, heavy cross to be built, which the strongest man of her time was hardly able to lift alone; and she too would have succumbed beneath its weight, had not the Mother of God in visible form mercifully assisted her to bear it, placing her ambrosial shoulder beside the earthly one.

These words the blond German did not use, but simpler ones, indeed so crude and uncouth that they could not be translated from a barbarian speech into our cultivated Tuscan without becoming boorish and grotesque; and that, my lords, would in turn be inappropriate to the expression of large-mindedness in the defiant blue eyes and the bold but shapely features of the girl whom I then saw before me.

"The story is credible!" I said to myself; for this feat by a barbarian queen seemed to me befitting the times and the customs of the dark close of the first millennium. "It might be true!"

"It is true!" Gertrude asserted curtly and vehemently, with a gloomy glance of conviction at the statuary, and

again made a move as if to depart; but I detained her for
the second time, with the question whether she were the
Gertrude of whom my guide of today, Hans of Splügen, had
told me. She replied in the affirmative, unabashed, not even
embarrassed, and a smile like a wandering light spread
slowly from the firm corners of her mouth over her brown
face, now beginning to grow pale in the convent air.

Then she reflected and said, " I knew that he would come
to my investiture, and I can have no objection. Seeing my
tresses fall will help him to forget me. Since you happen
to be here, reverend father, I will make a request of you.
If the man returns with you to Constance, reveal to him
the cause of my refusal to be his wife after " — and she
blushed, though almost imperceptibly — " after I had been
friendly with him in all honor, according to the custom of
our country. More than once I have been on the point of
telling him the story, but I bit my lip; for it is a secret
compact between the Mother of God and myself, and
secrets should not be disclosed. To you, however, who are
versed in secrets of the soul, I can confide the compact without betrayal. You shall then acquaint Hans with as much
of it as is fitting and to you seems meet. It is only that he
may not deem me fickle and ungrateful, and remember me
as such.

" This is how it is with me. When I was a mere child —
I was ten years old and had already lost my father —
mother was taken with a grave and hopeless sickness, and
fear came upon me, lest I be left alone in the world. Out
of this fear, and out of love for my mother, I dedicated
myself to the Virgin Mary for my twentieth year, if she
would preserve my mother's life until then, or nearly then.
She did so, and mother lived until last Corpus Christi day,
when she peacefully died, just at the time when Hans had
work as a carpenter in the convent; so that he it was who
made mother's coffin. Since I was now alone in the world,
what wonder is it that I fell in love with him? He is honest
and thrifty, as the Italians are for the most part; ' modest

and discreet,' as they say on the other side of the mountains. Moreover, we could converse in two languages; for
my father, who was a strong and courageous man, had
repeatedly accompanied a puny, timid tradesman, not without profit, over the mountains, and had brought home a few
bits of Italian from the other side. If now Hans called me
cara bambina, I returned the compliment by calling him
poverello, and both ring true, though I will find no fault
with the words of endearment usual in our country, when
they are honestly meant.

"But it was at this time also that I was due to keep my
vow, and every ringing of the Angelus reminded me of it.

"On the other hand, thoughts came into my mind and
whispered to me such things as ' The vow of an innocent
child who does not know the difference between man and
woman could have no power to bind you,' or ' Kind as she
is, the Virgin Mother would likely have granted you your
mother's life of her own mercy and as a free gift.' But I
said in reply, 'A bargain is a bargain,' and ' Honesty is
the best policy!' She has kept her part of the agreement,
and I will keep mine. Without truth and faith the world
cannot endure. What did my father say, who is no more?
' I would keep my word with the devil,' said he, ' not to
mention the Lord our God!'

"Hear now, reverend father, what I think and believe.
Since the Virgin Mother bore the cross for the queen, she
has, recruiting her convent, from time immemorial helped
all novices without distinction to bear it. It has become a
habit with her; she does it unconsciously. With my own
eyes I, a nine-year-old child, saw how Lieschen of Wein-
felden, a sickly creature who took the veil here, carried the
ponderous cross as if in sport on her drooping shoulder.

"Now I shall say to the Virgin, ' If thou wilt have me,
take me! — although I — if thou wert Gertrude and I were
the Mother of God — should perhaps not take a child at its
word. But no matter: a bargain is a bargain! — only with
this difference: the duchess, burdened with sins, felt re-

lieved and happy in the convent; it will be pain and sorrow for me. If thou bearest the cross for me, lighten my heart also; else there will be trouble, Mother of God! If thou canst not lighten my heart, then let me a thousand times rather to my shame and before the eyes of all the people plunge down and fall flat upon the floor!''

As I watched these laboring thoughts slowly draw deep furrows in Gertrude's young brow I smiled and suggested cunningly, ''An adroit and clever girl could extricate herself from the difficulty by stumbling!'' Then fire flashed from her blue eyes. '' Do you think, sir, I shall cheat? '' she exclaimed wrathfully. '' So help me God the Father, the Son, and the Holy Ghost in my last hour, as I will honestly bear the cross with all the strength and sinews of these my arms!'' And she raised her arms convulsively, as though she were already carrying the cross, so that the sleeves of her cowl and smock fell far back. Then I, as the Florentine that I am, beheld the slender, powerful, feminine arms with artistic delight. She observed me, frowned, and indignantly turned her back upon me.

After she had gone I seated myself in a confessional, rested upon my elbow, and meditated — verily not upon the barbarian maiden, but upon the Roman classic. Suddenly my heart rejoiced and I cried out exultantly, '' Thanks, ye immortal gods. A darling of the comic muse is restored to the world! Plautus is won!''

Friends, a conspiracy of circumstances guaranteed me this success.

I know not, Cosimo, what your views are on the subject of miracles. I myself am a tolerable believer, neither superstitious nor presumptuous; for I cannot endure those absolutists who, when an inexplicable fact has gathered an atmosphere of superstition about it, either summarily believe or just as summarily reject the whole phenomenon — moon and corona — without investigation and without distinction.

The marvel and the fraud, both I believed I had here discovered.

The heavy cross was genuine, and a magnificent sinner, a barbarian woman, might have lifted it with the super-human strength of despair and fervor. But this deed had not been repeated; on the contrary, it had for centuries been imitated by jugglery. Who was guilty of the fraud? Was it mistaken piety? Calculating avarice? The answer to these questions lay hidden in the darkness of the times. But so much was certain: the horrible cross, black with age, which was exhibited to the people, and the one which had been borne by a succession of simple or compliant novices — and only lately by the feeble and wily Lieschen of Wein-felden at her investiture — were two distinct pieces of wood; and all the while that the heavy one was being shown and weighed on the lawn, a light counterfeit was carefully locked up in some secret place within the convent, in order on the morrow to change places with the true one and deceive the eyes of the people.

The existence of a counterfeit cross, of which I was as much convinced as of my own existence, afforded me one weapon. A recent event afforded me another weapon.

Three dethroned popes and two heretics burned at the stake did not suffice to reform the church; the commissions of the Council were busied, one with this, the other with that abuse to be corrected. One of the commissions, of which the most Christian doctor Gerson and the stern Pierre d'Ailly were members and I for the time being was secretary, sought to restore discipline in the nunneries. Counterfeit miracles, dangerous in the unreliable hands of women, and the evil books read by the sisters came up for discussion. Be it said in passing: these matters were treated by the two Frenchmen with a degree of pedantry simply incomprehensible to us Italians, without the sug-gestion of a jest, howsoever readily one might have found the humor of the situation. Enough! The fact of these discussions formed the warp, sinful participation in a fraudulent miracle the woof of my fabric, and the net was woven which unexpectedly I cast over the head of the abbess.

Slowly I mounted the steps of the choir and from there turned to the right into the likewise lofty and boldly vaulted sacristy, in which, designated by self-glorifying inscriptions, the empty spot appeared where the heavy cross usually leaned against the wall, and whither it was destined presently to return from the convent lawn. Two small portals led into two side rooms. One proved to be locked. Opening the other, I stood in a room dimly lighted by a circular window obscured with cobwebs. Behold, it contained the convent library huddled together upon a few worm-eaten shelves.

My whole being throbbed with excitement, as though I were a youthful lover entering the chamber of Lydia or Glycera. With trembling hands and shaking knees I drew near to the parchments; and if I had found the Umbrian's comedies among them, I should have covered them with insatiable kisses.

But alas! I turned the leaves of naught but rituals and liturgies, the sacred contents of which gave cold comfort to my disappointment. No manuscript of Plautus! The report had been true. Instead of finding the buried treasure, a stupid collector had, by clumsy importunity, caused it to sink into unfathomable depths. I came upon — as my only booty — a dust-covered copy of the *Confessions of St. Augustine*, and as I have always been fond of the subtle little volume, I mechanically thrust it into my pocket, thus providing myself, according to my habit, with reading matter for the evening. Lo, like a bolt of lightning from a clear sky, my little abbess, who had had the cross dragged back to the sacristy and, without my having noticed her in the all-absorbing keenness of my desire and my disappointment, had trailed me through the open door into the library — like a bolt of lightning, I say, the little woman, cursing and railing, descended upon me; nay more, she groped with unseemly searching about my toga and brought to light again the church father reposing in my bosom.

"Mannikin," she shrieked, "I saw at once by your long

nose that you are one of those Italian martens which of
late have been sniffing around after books in our convents.
But I tell you there is a difference between a befuddled
monk of St. Gall and a nimble woman of Appenzell. I
know," she continued with a smirk, " what bacon draws the
cats. They are watching for an opportunity to seize the
buffoon's book which we have stored up here. No one of
us knew what was in it until the other day an Italian scamp
came to venerate our most holy relics and then tried to
carry off the jester under his long priestly gown,"—she
pointed to mine. " But I said to myself, ' Brigittchen of
Trogen, don't be swindled! The pigskin must be worth
its weight in gold, since the Italian risks his neck for it.'
For in our country, man, we say, ' He who steals a rope's
worth shall hang by the rope! ' Brigittchen, who is up to
snuff, privately consults a learned friend, a man without
guile, the priest of Diessenhofen, who is fond of our humble
wine and at times plays merry pranks upon our sisters.
After he had examined the odd scrolls, yellow with age, he
exclaimed, ' Odsnigs, Lady Abbess, you can get something
for that! You can build your convent a barn and a wine-
press! Take the book, my good woman, hide it under your
pillow, lie with the podex—so it is called—beneath you,
and by the crown of the Virgin stay there until an honest
purchaser presents himself!' And so Brigittchen did,
though she has lain somewhat uncomfortably ever since."

I suppressed a smile at the Umbrian's resting-place, to
which the three judges of the lower world may have consigned him for his sins, and, assuming the dignity which
I possess when circumstances call for it, I reproved her
with a stern glance.

"Abbess," I said in a solemn tone, " you do not know
who I am. Before you stands an emissary of the Council,
one of the fathers assembled in Constance, one of the holy
men commissioned to reform the nunneries." And I unfolded a splendidly engrossed bill of innkeeper's charges;
for I was inspired by the nearness of the comic poet in
hiding.

" In the name," I read, " and by authority of the seventeenth ecumenical council! Let no Christian vestal sully her hands with one of those works dangerous to good morals, whether composed in Latin or in one of the vulgar tongues, whereof the invention hath corrupted the souls of . . . Pious Mother Superior, I may not offend your chaste ears by reading the names of these reprobates. . . .

" Counterfeit miracles, traditional or once performed, we prosecute with inexorable severity. If intentional fraud can be proved, the guilty woman — though she were the abbess — shall without exception atone for the sacrilege by death in the flames."

The abbess became as white as a ghost. But with admirable presence of mind the hypocrite immediately recovered her composure.

" Glory and honor to God! " she cried, " for finally setting His holy church in order! " And with an ingratiating smirk she fetched from a corner of the bookcase a daintily bound little volume. " This," she said, " an Italian cardinal, our guest, left behind for us. He used to read himself to sleep with it after dinner. The priest of Diessenhofen, who examined it, pronounced the opinion that it was the grossest and most damnable thing that had been conceived since the invention of the alphabet — and that too by a cleric. Pious father, I confide this abomination to your keeping. Free me from its contagion! " And she handed over to me — my *Facetiæ!*

Although this surprise was probably due to the malicious mischief-making of chance rather than of the Mother Superior, I felt hurt and indignant. I began to hate the little abbess. For our writings are our own flesh and blood, and I flattered myself that in mine I walk demurely, offending neither the modest muses nor the infallible church.

" It is well," I said. " I only wish you might be found guiltless in the second and more essential point! To the assembled people you have, in the neighborhood and under the very eyes of the Council," I remarked reproachfully,

" promised a miracle with so much vulgar advertising that you cannot now withhold the performance. I do not know whether that was wise. Do not marvel, abbess, that your miracle is going to be put to the test! You have invited your own doom!"

The woman's knees knocked together and her eyes wandered. "Follow me," I said sternly, "and let us inspect the instruments of the miracle!"

She followed in dismay and we entered the sacristy, to which the genuine cross had returned, and with its rifts and cracks and gigantic shadow in the spacious dimness of the noble room was resting as mightily on the wall as if only today a despairing great sinner had seized it and had sunk to her knees under its weight, touching the stone pavement with her forehead at the moment when the Queen of Heaven appeared and succored her. I tried to raise it, but could not lift it an inch. All the more ridiculous did the outrage appear, of replacing this crushing burden with a bauble. I turned resolutely toward the high narrow door behind which I suspected the latter to be.

"The key, abbess," I commanded. The little woman stared at me with eyes of horror, but boldly answered, "Lost, my lord bishop, more than ten years ago."

"Woman," I rejoined with terrible seriousness, "your life is at stake! Yonder dwells a retainer of my friend the count of Doccaburgo. Thither I shall send or go for help. If there be found here a counterfeit copy of the real cross, of lighter weight, you shall be consumed by flames of fire, you sinner, like the heretic Huss, and not less guilty than he!"

There was a moment of silence. Then the woman — I know not whether with chattering teeth or with gnashing of teeth — drew forth an antique key with complicated wards and opened the door. The result was flattering — my intelligence had not deceived me. There against the wall of the high, chimney-like room leaned a black cross with rifts and cracks, which I at once grasped and in my feeble arms lifted without difficulty. In every one of its bumps and hollows, in all details the counterfeit conformed to the model of the genuine cross, and even for a sharp eye was indistinguishable from it — only that it was ten times lighter. Whether it was hollowed out or constructed of cork or some other light material, the rush and tumble of events never permitted me to ascertain.

I admired the perfection of the imitation and the thought dawned upon me that only a great artist, only an Italian could have brought this to pass; and, enthusiastic as I am for the fame of my native land, I exclaimed, "Perfect! Masterly!" — verily, extolling not the fraud, but the art expended upon it.

With a grin, the brazen woman, who had watched me attentively, shook her finger at me and said, "Crafty joker, you have outwitted me, and I know what there will be to pay! Take your jester, whom I will fetch at once, under your arm, keep your own counsel, and God be with you on your way!" Whenever, on one of the seven hills of Rome, two augurs met and, according to an ancient saying, smiled knowingly at each other, the play of features was surely more delicate than the gross laugh which distorted the face of my abbess and was translatable into the cynical words, "We all know where Bartolo gets his wine. We are rogues all together, and no one needs to put on airs."

But meanwhile I was pondering over a punishment for the worthless woman.

Then in the silence that had suddenly ensued we heard a tripping, a whispering and tittering in the adjacent choir and surmised that we were being watched by the idle and inquisitive nuns. "By my precious maidenhood," the woman implored me, "let us go, my lord bishop! Not for the wealth of the world would I have my nuns find me here with you; for you are a handsome man and my sisters' tongues are as sharp as scissors and knives!" This scruple seemed to me well founded. I bade her depart and take her nuns with her.

After a while I too left the sacristy. But I only carefully closed the door of the room in which the sham cross was concealed, without turning the key. This I drew out, put it beneath my cloak, and let it slip into a crevice between two stalls in the choir, where, for all I know, it may still repose to this very day. I did this, however, with no definite plan, but prompted by some whispering god or goddess.

When I sat in the low-studded prioress's room, alone with my abbess and an odor of sanctity, I experienced such a longing for the innocent play of the muse and such a repugnance for the twists and turns of entrapped mendacity that I determined to make short work of the matter. The Mother Superior had to confess to me how she had been initiated into the hoary swindle, and I closed the incident with few pretorian edicts. She confessed that her predecessor in office had, when at the point of death, called her and the father confessor into secret conference, and that both had commended the inherited sham miracle to her fostering care as the economic salvation of the convent. The confessor, she volubly related, had been inexhaustible in praise of the venerable age of the fraud, its deep meaning, and instructiveness. Better and more convincingly than any sermon, he said, the phantom miracle symbolized to the people the initial difficulty and the subsequent ease of a godly life. This symbolism had so turned the head of the poor woman that in one and the same breath she affirmed that she had committed no wrong and that as a child she too had once been honest.

"I will spare you for the sake of our Mother Church, upon which the flame of your burning at the stake would cast a false light"—with these words I cut short her rustic logic, and curtly commanded her to give the counterfeit cross to the flames after the loudly trumpeted miracle had been performed once more—from motives of prudence I did not venture to prevent this—but to deliver the Plautus without delay.

Scolding and reviling me, the abbess obeyed. She submitted to the decrees of the Council of Constance as they were formulated by me, not indeed with the foreknowledge of the assembled fathers, but certainly in their spirit and in conformity to their intention.

When Brigittchen, growling like a bear, brought me the codex — I had fled to a comfortable room in the visitors' quarters situated next the wall that encircled the convent — I forced her ill-bred ladyship out of the apartment and locked myself in with the Umbrian's comic characters. Not a sound disturbed me there, except the refrain of a children's song which some peasant girls were singing in the meadow beneath my window, and this made my solitude only the more enjoyable.

After a while, to be sure, the Mother Superior, highly excited, made a great pother outside, and with desperate fists pounded upon the heavy bolted oaken door, demanding the key to the open room of the counterfeit cross. I gave her, with my regrets, the brief and veritable information that it was not in my hands, paid no further attention to her, and, myself in the seventh heaven of delight, let the miserable woman wail and groan like a soul in Purgatory. But I reveled as one bidden to a wedding feast.

A classic author newly come to light — not an obscure thinker, nor a sublime poet — no, that which lies nearest at hand and eternally fascinates, the wide, wide world, the pulse of life, the hilarious market-places of Rome and Athens, wit, altercation, and equivocation, the passions, the effrontery of human nature in the extenuating exaggeration of the comic mirror. While I devoured one piece I was already keeping hungry watch over the next.

I had finished the witty *Amphitruo*, the *Aulularia* with the incomparable figure of the miser lay open before me — but I stopped and leaned back in my chair; for my eyes pained me. Twilight and darkness were coming on. The girls in the meadow outside had for at least a quarter of an hour indefatigably repeated the silly ditty,

" Adam, he had seven sons   *   *   * "

Now they mischievously struck up a new refrain, and
with droll resoluteness they sang,

"To the convent I'll not go,
"I'll not be a nun, no, no!"

I leaned out in order to catch sight of these little foes
of celibacy and take pleasure in the contemplation of their
innocence. But their game was in no wise an innocent one.
Nudging each other with their elbows, and exchanging
knowing glances, they sang, not without invidiousness and
malice, up at a grated window, behind which they supposed
Gertrude to be. Or was she already kneeling in the sacristy
yonder, under the pale glimmer of the ever-burning light,
according to the custom of those about to take the veil,
who pass in prayer the night before their marriage to
heaven? But what was that to me? I lighted the lamp
and began to read the comedy of the Pot.

Not until my lamp burned out and the letters swam before
my weary eyes did I throw myself down upon my couch
and fall into a restless slumber. Soon the comic characters
were again hovering about me. Here a soldier boasted
with high-sounding words, there the drunken youth caressed
his sweetheart, who with a graceful turn of her head met
his kisses half way. Then, without warning, there stood
in the midst of the merry antique rabble a broad-shouldered,
barefoot barbarian maiden girdled with a rope, brought
like a slave to the mart, staring at me, as it seemed, with
reproachful and threatening eyes that gleamed forth from
beneath her gloomy brow.

I was frightened and awoke with a start. The morning
dawned. On account of the summer sultriness I had left
one half of the little window open, and from the adjacent
choir of the convent chapel I heard a monotonous orison
that passed over into a smothered groan and then into a
violent outcry.

Interrupting himself, the narrator turned to a grave man
who sat over against him and, in spite of the summer heat,

had after the manner of the ancients draped the folds of his mantle about him. "My learned and far-famed friend," said he, "my great philosopher, tell me, I beseech you, what is conscience?

Is it a universal attribute? By no means. We have all known men who had none, and, to mention only one, our holy father, John XXIII., whom we dethroned at Constance, had no conscience, but on the contrary, such a happy heart, such a cheerful, I had almost said childlike spirit, that in the midst of his evil deeds no spectre disturbed his slumbers and he awoke every morning more serene than he had lain down the day before. When at the castle of Gottlieben, where he was confined, I unfolded the scroll of complaints against him and with hesitant voice and flushed face read to him the sum of his sins — ten times greater than the number attached to his papal name, *scelera horrenda, abominanda* — he picked up a pen and to while away the time adorned a St. Barbara in his breviary with a moustache.

No, conscience is no universal attribute, and even among us, who have a conscience, it appears as a Proteus, in changing forms. In your humble servant, for example, it awakes every time that it can embody itself in an image or in a tone. When recently I was a guest at the court of one of those petty tyrants with whom our fortunate Italy swarms, and on that balmy evening sat to wine and music with fair women on an airy balcony that jutted out from the tower of the castle over a bottomless pool of cool water, I heard a sigh from below. It was the voice of a prisoner. Banished was my joy, and I could remain there no longer. It troubled my conscience to enjoy life, kissing, drinking, and laughing so near to misery.

In the same manner I could not now endure the cry of a woman in despair so close at hand. I threw a cloak about me and stole through the dim cloister to the choir, saying to myself that while I was reading Plautus a change

must have come over Gertrude: on the threshold of a decision she must have come to the incontrovertible conviction
that she should surely perish in this community, in the
nothingness — or worse, the corruption of the convent, confined as she should be together with the common herd,
despising it and hated in her turn.

In the portal of the sacristy I stopped to listen, and saw
Gertrude wringing her hands before the genuine, heavy
cross. Believe me, they were bleeding, and I daresay her
knees were bleeding too; for she had been upon her knees
in prayer the whole night long; her voice was hoarse, and
her converse with God, after her heart had sunk within her
and no new words came to her lips, was convulsive and
brutish, like a dying effort.

" Mary, Mother of God," she cried, " have mercy on me!
Let me fall beneath the weight of thy cross; it is too heavy
for me! I shudder at the thought of a cell! " And she
made a motion as if she were snatching or uncoiling a serpent from about her body; and then, in a paroxysm of
anguish, even suppressing her shame, she exclaimed,
" What befits me is sun and cloud, sickel and scythe, husband and child . . . "

In the midst of this misery I could not restrain a smile
at this human confession made to the Blessed Virgin; but
the smile died on my lips. Gertrude had suddenly jumped
to her feet and fixed her great eyes, weirdly staring from
out her blanched face, upon a spot in the wall which was
marred by I know not what red stain.

" Mary, Mother of God, have mercy on me! " she cried
again. " My limbs cannot abide in the cell and I shall
strike my head against the ceiling. Let me sink under the
weight of thy cross; it is too heavy for me! But if thou
shouldst make it light upon my shoulder without being able
to make light my heart, then beware " — and she stared at
the uncanny spot — " lest some morning they find me lying
with a crushed head at the foot of the wall! " Infinite
compassion seized me — and not compassion alone, but
anxious apprehension also.

Exhausted, Gertrude had seated herself upon a chest which contained some sacred relic, and was plaiting her blond hair which, during her wrestling with God, had loosened itself from the braids. At the same time she sang to herself half sadly, half playfully, not in her robust alto, but in a high-pitched child's voice not her own,

> "To the convent I must run,
> Must be a poor, unhappy nun . . ."

paraphrasing that refrain with which the peasant children had derided her.

This was madness, which sought to waylay her and slip with her into the cell. But Optimus Maximus availed himself of me as the instrument of his will and bade me save Gertrude at any cost.

Now I, too, addressed myself in unfeigned piety to that virgin goddess whom the ancients adored as Pallas Athena and whom we call Mary. "Whoever thou art," I prayed with uplifted hands, "Wisdom, as some say, Mercy, as others affirm — it is all one; Wisdom doth not record the vow of an inexperienced child, nor will Mercy hold an adult woman bound by the foolish promise of an infant. With a smile of clemency thou wilt annul this empty bond. It is thy cause I plead, goddess. Be gracious unto me!"

Since I had given the abbess, who feared treachery, my word that I should have no further speech with Gertrude, I determined after the manner of the ancients with three symbolical actions to bring the truth home to the novice, so manifestly that even the slow wits of a peasant girl could grasp it.

Paying no attention to Gertrude, I stepped up to the cross. "When I wish to recognize an object that I have once seen, I put my mark on it," I said pedantically; and drawing my sharp dagger, forged by our famous fellow-citizen, Pantaleone Ubbriaco the cutler, I cut a chip of some size out from under the head and the cross-beam, as it were the arm-pit of the cross.

Secondly, I took five measured steps. Then I burst out laughing and began with expressive gesticulation, "That porter in the hall at Constance cut a comical figure when my luggage arrived! He surveyed the biggest piece there was, an enormous box, rolled his sleeves above his elbows, spat upon his hands — the rude fellow — and, straining every muscle for a supreme effort, raised the trifling burden of an empty chest with ease to his deluded shoulder. Ha! Ha! Ha!"

Thirdly and lastly, I placed myself in mock solemnity between the real cross and the sham cross in its unlocked abiding place, and repeatedly pointing this way and that, I oracularly murmured, "Truth in the air, falsehood in there!" — presto! and I clapped my hands, "Falsehood i' the air, truth is in there!"

Out of the corner of my eye I looked over at the novice sitting in the twilight, in order to gather from the facial expression of the young barbarian the effect of these three oracles upon her. I perceived the tension of disquieting meditation and the first flicker of blazing wrath.

Then I repaired to my room, cautiously, as I had gone forth from it, threw myself without undressing upon my couch, and enjoyed the sweet slumber of a good conscience until aroused by the hum of the multitude proceeding to the convent and by the clangor of the festal bells above my head.

When I again entered the sacristy, Gertrude, deathly pale, as though she were being led to the scaffold, was just returning from a procession to a neighboring chapel, a traditional requirement no doubt instituted to give opportunity for the fraudulent exchange of crosses. The adornment of the bride of heaven began. In the group of psalm-singing nuns the novice girded herself with the coarse, thrice-knotted rope and slowly removed the shoes from her sinewy but well-shapen feet. Now they presented to her the crown of thorns. This, by contrast to the symbolical counterfeit cross, was a wreath of hard, real thorns, bristling with sharp points. Gertrude seized it eagerly and pressed it with voluptuous cruelty so firmly upon her head that the warm rain of her young blood spurted forth and in heavy drops ran down her innocent brow. Sublime wrath, a present judgment of the righteous God, gleamed destruction in the blue eyes of the peasant girl; so that the nuns began to recoil from her in fear. Six of their number, whom the abbess had presumably initiated into the pious fraud, now laid the sham cross upon her honest shoulder, with clumsy grimaces, as though they were hardly able to lift the bauble, and with such stupid hypocrisy that I verily believed I saw the truth of God in the thorny crown, openly honored and glorified by human untruthfulness, but secretly reviled.

Now everything developed with the swiftness of a thunderstorm. Gertrude cast a quick glance at the place where on the genuine cross my dagger had cut a deep mark, and found the false one unscarred. Contemptuously she let the light cross glide from her shoulder, without clasping it in her arms. Then with a shriek of derisive laughter she seized it again, and triumphantly smote it to pieces upon the stone pavement. And with a bound she stood before the door of the room in which the real, the heavy cross was concealed, opened the door, found and lifted the cross, shouted wildly for joy, as though she had discovered a treasure, raised the cross unaided to her shoulder, embraced it exultantly with her valiant arms, and turned with her burden slowly toward the choir where, as upon an open stage, she was to appear before the multitude. Breathlessly waiting, nobility, clergy, peasantry, a whole people, crowded the spacious nave of the church. Lamenting, reproving, threatening, imploring, the abbess with her nuns threw herself in the way.

But she, with gleaming eyes lifted up to heaven, cried out, " Now, Mother of God, do thou conclude this business honestly! " And then with a loud voice, " Make way! " — like a workman carrying a piece of timber through a press of people.

All gave way before her and she entered the choir, where, with a vicar of the bishop at their head, the rural clergy awaited her. All eyes were focussed upon the heavy-laden shoulder and the blood-besprinkled countenance. But the true cross proved too heavy for Gertrude and no goddess made it lighter. She strode with panting bosom, ever more bent and more slowly, as though her bare feet were implanted and rooted in the floor. She stumbled a little, recovered her balance, stumbled again, sank down upon her left knee, then upon her right, and endeavored with all her might to rise again. It was in vain. Now her left hand let go the cross and, stretched forward to reach the floor, supported for a moment the weight of her entire body. Then the arm bent at the elbow and doubled up. The head with its crown of thorns fell forward heavily and struck the stone pavement with a thud. Over the body of the exhausted victim the cross rolled ponderously, released by the right hand only after Gertrude had been stunned by the fall.

That was bloody truth, not the illusion of jugglery. One sigh rose from the breasts of a thousand witnesses.

The horrified nuns drew Gertrude forth from beneath the cross and lifted her to her feet. She had swooned in her fall, but consciousness soon returned to the sturdy maiden. She passed her hand over her forehead. Her eye fell upon the cross which had overwhelmed her. A smile of thanks flitted across her face, to the goddess whose help had not been forthcoming. Then with heavenly humor she spoke the roguish words, " Thou dost not wish me, Virgin pure! Then another will have me!"

Still wearing the crown of thorns, without appearing to feel the bloody pricks, she now set her foot upon the first of the steps that led from the choir down into the nave. At the same time her eyes wandered searchingly about the congregation, and found him, whom they sought for. A profound silence ensued. " Hans of Splügen," Gertrude began in clear and audible tones, " wilt thou take me for

thy wedded wife?" "Indeed, I will, with joy a thousand-
fold. Come down and see!" answered a happy and convincing masculine voice from the back of the nave.

She did so and descended calmly, but radiant with joy,
one step after another, once more the simple peasant, who
no doubt was glad soon to forget the affecting spectacle that
in her despair she had given the multitude, now that her
modest human desire was granted and she was permitted
to return to the every-day sphere of her humble existence.
Laugh at me, if you will, Cosimo; I was disappointed. For
a short space the peasant girl had appeared to my excited
senses as the incarnation of a higher being, as a demonic
creature, as Truth exultantly unmasking Falsehood. But
"What is truth?" asked Pilate.

Pondering this and following Gertrude from the choir
down into the nave, I was plucked in the sleeve by my messenger, who informed me of the sudden election of Otto
Colonna to the papacy by enthusiastic acclamation, and of
sundry remarkable circumstances.

When I looked up again, Gertrude had vanished. But
the excited multitude was shouting and clamoring with
divided opinion. From yonder group of men the words
resounded, "Hag! Witch!" They meant the abbess. Here
women's voices shrilled, "Sinner! Impudent hussy!" That
was Gertrude. Whether the former surmised the pious
fraud, or the latter believed the miracle to be desecrated
by Gertrude's worldliness,—no matter; in either case the
spell of the relic was broken and the career of the miracle
closed.

Coarsely reviled by the people, the valiant Brigittchen
began to retort in kind, and the dumbfounded faces of
the attending priests showed a complete scale of expressions from sly complicity down to the most incorruptible
stupidity.

I felt my dignity as a cleric and put an end to the abomination. Mounting the pulpit, I solemnly announced to
assembled Christendom, "*Habemus pontificem Dominum*

Othonem Colonna! " and struck up a resounding *Te Deum*, in which first the chorus of nuns and then the entire congregation lustily joined. After the hymn had been sung, nobles and peasants hastened to mount their horses or to set out afoot on the way to Constance, where, after the *triregnum* had come to an end, the blessing conveyed to the city and to the world must be trebly strong.

I, for my part, slipped back into the cloister in order with all secrecy to get the Plautus that was in my room. Going furtively away again, with the codex under my arm, I happened upon the abbess who, economical as she was, was carefully carrying the pieces of the sham cross in a great basket to the kitchen. I congratulated her upon the *dénouement*. But Brigittchen believed herself swindled and yelled at me in fury, " Go to the devil, you two Italian scoundrels," meaning, so far as I could judge, the Umbrian Marcus Accius Plautus and the Tuscan Poggio Bracciolini, your fellow-citizen. A pretty blond boy, another curly-head, whom Hans of Splügen, before his departure with Gertrude, had thoughtfully engaged for me, then led out my mule, which carried me back to Constance.

Plaudite amici! My story is at an end. When the Council of Constance, which lasted longer than this little narrative, was likewise at an end, I returned with my gracious master, His Holiness Martin V., over the mountains, and found as our host and hostess in the inn at Splügen, to the north of the dangerous pass, Hänsel and Gertrude in health and prosperity — she not in a stifling cell but in a wind-swept rocky valley, with a child at her breast and the conjugal cross resting lightly upon her shoulder.

Let this *Facetia inedita*, illustrious Cosimo, be a not unwelcome supplement to the codex of Plautus which at this hour I present to you, or rather to our native land, whose Father you are, and to learning, to which ycur halls with their store of treasures are always open.

It was my intention to bequeath the unique manuscript
to you, lest, as a living donor, I should invite the tenfold
greater recompense with which you are wont in your incor-
rigible generosity to reward every gift presented to you
in homage. But who knows — Poggio sighed resignedly —
whether my sons would respect my last will? "

Cosimo replied amiably, " I thank you for both, your
Plautus and your *Facetia.* Without a scruple you lived
this and accomplished it, young as you then were. As a
mature man you have recounted it to us in the wisdom of
your years. This toast " — he lifted a noble bowl enclasped
by a laughing satyr — " I pledge to my honest Poggio and
his blond barbarian maiden ! "

They drank and laughed. Then the conversation passed
quickly from Plautus to the thousand discovered treasures
and unrolled parchments of antiquity, and to the greatness
of the century.

THE MONK'S MARRIAGE

was in Verona. Before an ample fire that filled a spacious fireplace, youthful courtiers of both sexes were gathered in the most comfortable attitudes consistent with good breeding about a sovereign as youthful as any, and two fair women. On the left of the hearth sat this princely group, which the retinue joined in a quarter circle, leaving the other side of the hearth, in accordance with courtly custom, quite unoccupied. The ruler was that Scaliger whom they called Cangrande. Of the ladies between whom he sat, the one leaning somewhat backward into the semi-darkness next to the hearth appeared to be his wife, the other, in the full glare of the light, might have been a relative or friend; and there were stories told to the accompaniment of significant glances and suppressed laughter.

There now stepped into this voluptuous and wanton circle a grave man whose noble features and flowing garments seemed to mark him as coming from another world. "My lord, I come to warm myself by your fireside," said the stranger—half solemnly and half contemptuously, disdaining to add that in spite of the frosty November evening the careless servants had forgotten or neglected to make a fire in the guest chamber situated on one of the upper floors.

"Sit down beside me, my Dante," replied Cangrande. "But if you desire the warmth of good fellowship, forbear to gaze as is your wont mutely into the flames! We are telling stories, and the hand that today has been forging tercets — mounting to my astrological chamber I heard some one in your apartment scanning verses in a mumbling sing-song — this mighty hand must today not refuse to take in its fingers the plaything of a merry tale, without crushing it. Dismiss the goddesses " — he meant to say the muses — " and enjoy yourself with these fair mortals." With a casual gesture Scaliger indicated to his guest the two ladies, of whom the taller, sitting with apparent indifference in the shadow, had no idea of moving, whereas the smaller — a sprightly person — readily made room for the Florentine beside her. He, however, did not act upon his host's invitation, but proudly chose the last seat, at the other end of the line. He was either displeased with the prince's bigamy — though it were but the sport of an evening — or disgusted with the court fool who with outstretched legs was sitting beside Cangrande's armchair, on the prince's mantle which had slipped down to the floor.

The fool, a toothless old fellow with staring eyes and flabby, babbling, candy-smeared lips — except Dante the only aged man in the company — was called Gocciola, that is "Dropkin," because he used always to drain the last sirupy drops from the empty glasses; and he hated the stranger with childish malice; for he saw in Dante his rival for the favor of his not very discriminating master. He made a grimace, and with a scornful grin impudently directed the attention of the pretty neighbor on his left to the poet's profile projected upon the illuminated ceiling of the lofty apartment. Dante's silhouette resembled a gigantic woman with a long hooked nose and protruding under-lip, a Fate or the like. The vivacious girl suppressed a childlike laugh. Her neighbor, a keen-eyed youth named Ascanio, helped her smother it by turning to Dante with that discreet reverence with which he liked to be addressed.

"Do not disdain, Homer and Virgil of Italy," he entreated, "to mingle in our innocent amusement. Descend to our level, master, and tell a story, instead of singing."

"What is your theme?" queried Dante, less uncompanionably than at first, but still gruffly enough.

"Sudden change of calling," answered the youth briefly, "with good, or evil, or comical result."

Dante reflected. His melancholy eyes surveyed the company, which was made up in a way that seemed not altogether to displease him; for he discovered in it, along with many a shallow pate, some heads of notable distinction. "Has any one of you treated the unfrocked monk?" he remarked, already more kindly disposed.

"Certainly, Dante," answered a warrior of frank and open mien, Germano by name, who wore a coat of chain-armor, was adorned with a drooping moustache, and pronounced his Italian with a slight German accent. "I myself told of young Manuccio, who leaped over the wall of his monastery in order to become a soldier."

"He acted rightly," Dante explained. "He had deceived himself as to his native bent."

"I, master," said in a gossiping tone a forward, somewhat luxurious woman of Padua, named Isotta, "have told of Helena Manente, who had just sacrificed the first lock of her hair to the consecrated shears, but quickly protected the other locks with both hands and choked back her monastic vow; for among the people in the nave of the church she had caught a glimpse of her friend, who had been taken into paynim slavery, had been most miraculously rescued, and now "—she was about to say, "hung his broken chains on the wall;" but her chatter was interrupted by Dante's words.

"She did well," said he, "for she acted in faithful obedience to her lovelorn nature. Hereof I now in nowise speak, but of an entirely different case: suppose, namely, that a monk, not of his own motion, not from awakened worldly desire or lust of conquest, not because he has not known himself, but for another's sake, under the pressure of another's will — though it were perhaps from motives of sacred loyalty — becomes recreant to himself even more than to the church, breaks vows that he has made to himself, and casts off a cowl that has fit his body and has never been irksome. Has this story been told? No? Very well; then I will relate it. But tell me, my patron and protector—how does such a matter end?" He had turned exclusively to Cangrande.

"Necessarily ill," replied the prince, without stopping to reflect. "He leaps well who may take a running start; but he who is thrust forward falls on the other side."

"You speak the truth, my lord," said Dante in confirmation, "and no other is the meaning of the apostle, if I understand him, when he writes that sin is whatsoever is not of faith, that is, is not of conviction and proceedeth not from the truth of our nature."

"'Must there then be monks in the world?'" tittered a subdued voice in the semi-obscurity of the corner, as if to say that any rescue from a manifestly unnatural state is a benefaction.

This reckless and heretical utterance gave no offense here; for at this court the freest speech concerning ecclesiastical affairs was tolerated, even smilingly fostered, while a frank or merely incautious word concerning the ruler, his person or his policy, might be fatal.

Dante's eye peered after the speaker and discovered him in the person of a high-born young cleric whose fingers were fondling the jeweled cross which he wore over his priestly garb.

"Not so far as I am concerned," answered the Florentine deliberately. "Let the monks die out as soon as a generation arises knowing how to unite the two supreme faculties of the human soul, justice and mercy, which seem mutually exclusive. Until that late hour comes in the history of the world, let the state administer one, and the church the other. Inasmuch, however, as the exercise of mercy demands a thoroughly unselfish soul, the three monastic vows are justified; for, as experience teaches, it is less difficult to renounce pleasure altogether than in part."

" But are there not more bad monks than good ones? " asked the clerical doubter further.

" No," Dante affirmed, " not with due regard to human frailty. Otherwise there must be more unrighteous judges than righteous ones, more cowardly than courageous warriors, more bad men than good."

" And is not that the case? " whispered he in the shadow.

" No," said Dante decidedly, and a heavenly transfiguration illumined his stern features. " Does not our philosophy inquire and seek to learn how evil came into the world? If the wicked were in the majority, we should inquire how good came into the world."

These proud and dark sayings imposed their authority upon the company, but at the same time aroused apprehension, lest the Florentine might become absorbed in his scholasticism instead of his story.

Cangrande saw his young favorite trying to prevent a pretty little yawn. Under these circumstances he came forward with the question, " Will you tell us a true story, my Dante, based upon documentary evidence, or a tale taken from popular tradition? Or is it to be an invention springing from your own laureate head? "

" I shall develop my story from an epitaph," replied Dante with solemn deliberateness.

" From an epitaph? "

" From an epitaph that I read years ago in the Franciscan monastery at Padua. The stone upon which it was inscribed lay in a corner of the monastery garden, concealed, to be sure, by luxuriant rose-bushes, but still within reach of the novices, if they crawled on their hands and knees and could bear a few scratches of the thorns on their cheeks. I commanded the prior — or rather, I requested him to have the stone in question transferred to the library and committed to the care of a man of years."

"What, then, did the inscription say?" asked the prince's consort in a tone of indifference.

"The inscription," Dante replied, "was in Latin and read, *Hic jacet monachus Astorre cum uxore Antiope. Sepeliebat Azzolinus.*"

"What does that mean?" asked the lady curiously.

Cangrande translated fluently, "Here rests Astorre the monk beside his wife Antiope. Ezzelino buried them."

"The abominable tyrant!" exclaimed the sentimental princess. "I am sure he had them buried alive because they loved each other, and heaped scorn upon his victim even in the grave by calling her the wife of the monk. He was cruel enough!"

"Hardly," Dante opined. "This matter has shaped itself otherwise in my mind and your interpretation is also improbable according to history; for Ezzelino menaced obedience to the church rather than the breaking of monastic vows. I take *sepeliebat* in a good sense: He gave both a burial."

"That is right," cried Cangrande joyfully. "You think as I do, Florentine. Ezzelino was a born ruler and, as such men are, was somewhat rough and violent. Nine-tenths of his crimes are the invention of priests and the story-loving populace."

"I would it were so!" sighed Dante. "As he appears in the plot of my story, I must say that he is not as yet the monster truly or falsely depicted in the chronicle, but that his cruelty is only just beginning to grave its sign, so to speak, in a wrinkle about his mouth — "

"A commanding figure," Cangrande warmly completed the portrait, "with bristling black hair over his forehead, as you depict him, a dweller in hell, in your twelfth canto. Where did you get your idea of that head of black hair?"

"It is your head," boldly answered Dante; and Cangrande felt flattered.

"The other figures in my story as well," he continued, with a smile, though threateningly, "I shall take, you will

permit me? " — and he turned to those sitting about him —
" from this company and give them your names; your
characters I shall not touch, for I cannot read beneath the
surface."

" My mien is at your service," said the princess with a
lordly air, her indifference beginning to wane.

A murmur of the utmost excitement ran through the circle
of auditors, and " Your story, Dante! " they breathed on
all sides, " Your story! "

" Here it is," said he, and told as follows:

Where the course of the Brenta in a graceful curve
approaches but does not touch the city of Padua, a bark
adorned with garlands and filled to overflowing with a
festive company glided on a heavenly summer day to the
music of muted flutes upon its swift but noiseless water.
It was the bridal party of Umberto Vicedomini and Diana
Pizzaguerra. The Paduan had gone to fetch his bride
from a convent situated on the upper course of the river,
whither, by virtue of an old custom of the city, maidens
of rank were wont to withdraw for the sake of religious
exercises before marriage. She sat on a purple cushion
in the middle of the boat between the bridegroom and his
three rosy-cheeked sons by his first marriage. Umberto
Vicedomini had buried the wife of his youth five years
before, when pestilence raged in Padua, and, although in
the full vigor of manhood, he had only painfully and reluctantly yielded to the daily urging of his old and sickly father
and resolved upon this second marriage.

With oars drawn in, the bark drifted, yielding to the
will of the stream. The boatmen accompanied the soft
music with a low chanty. Then suddenly both music and
song ceased. All eyes had turned toward the right bank,
where a splendid horseman drew in his steed and with a
wide sweep of his hand waved a greeting to those in the
bark. A shy murmur passed from thwart to thwart. The
oarsmen snatched their red caps from their heads and the

entire ship's company rose in fear and reverence, even the bridegroom, Diana, and the boys. With submissive gestures, waving of arms and half-bended knees, they turned toward the strand with such impetuosity and immoderate movement that the bark became unbalanced, listed to starboard, and suddenly overturned. A cry of horror, a whirling eddy, a vacant space in the middle of the stream which became dotted with bodies emerging only to sink again, and with floating garlands from the foundered bark! Help was not far to seek; for a short distance down-stream there was a small river port where fishermen and ferrymen dwelt, and where today the horses and litters were waiting to convey the company now perishing in the stream the rest of the way to Padua.

The first boats of rescuers put out from opposite shores. In one stood beside an old ferryman with a bushy beard, Ezzelino, the tyrant of Padua, the innocent cause of the calamity; in the other, coming from the left bank, a young monk and his ferryman, who was rowing the dusty pilgrim over the stream at the very moment when the accident occurred. The two boats met mid-way. Between them there floated in the river something resembling a wealth of blond hair, which with outstretched arm the monk resolutely seized, kneeling, while his boatsman, bracing himself, leaned backward as far as possible over the other side of the skiff. Grasping a thick tress, the monk lifted out of the swirling waters first a head, in which the eyes were closed, and then, with the aid of Ezzelino who had come close up to him, the body of a woman heavy with dripping garments. The tyrant had leaped from his skiff into the other and now contemplated the head, inanimate but retaining an expression of defiance and unhappiness, with a kind of rapt admiration, either of the distinguished features or of the peacefulness of death.

" Do you know her, Astorre? " he asked the monk. The latter shook his head, and Ezzelino continued, " See, it is your brother's wife."

The monk cast a shy glance of compassion upon the pale face, and presently the slumbering eyes slowly opened.

"Take her ashore," Ezzelino commanded. But the monk committed her to the care of his ferryman. "I will search for my brother," he cried, "until I find him." "I will help you, monk," said the tyrant, "but I doubt our being able to save him. I saw him embrace his sons and, enclasped by the three, sink hopelessly into the depths."

Meanwhile the Brenta had become covered with craft of all sorts. People cast about with poles, gaffs, hooks, nets, and in the quickly changing scene the figure of the ruler was everywhere at once, dominating the searchers and the burdens they raised.

"Come, monk," he said finally, "there is nothing more for you to do here. Umberto and his boys have now been lying too long on the bottom ever to come back to life. The current has dragged them away. It will cast them up upon the shore when it has wearied of them. But do you see the tents yonder?" A number of these had been pitched along the bank of the Brenta for the reception of the expected wedding party, and now the dead or apparently dead were laid out in them, surrounded by lamenting relatives and servants who had already arrived in haste from the adjacent city. "There, monk, do what pertains to your office: works of charity! Comfort the living! Bury the dead!"

The monk had stepped ashore and had lost sight of the Imperial Governor. Out of the throng Diana came toward him, his brother's bride and widow, disconsolate, but again in possession of her senses. Her heavy hair was still dripping, but the drops fell upon a changed garment: a compassionate woman of the people had in the tent given up her own gown and taken possession of the costly wedding dress. "Pious brother," said Diana, turning to Astorre, "I have been left behind. The litter intended for me has in the confusion returned to the city with another, living or dead. Conduct me to the house of my father-in-law, who is your father."

The young widow was mistaken. Not in the consternation and confusion, but because of cowardice and superstition the servants of old Vicedomini had left her unattended. They were afraid to convey to the irascible old man a widow, and with her the news of the downfall of his house.

Since the monk saw many of his kind busied within and without the tents with works of charity, he acceded to the request. " Let us go," he said, and started with the young woman for the city, whose towers and cupolas loomed ever larger on the background of blue sky. The way was crowded with hundreds of people, hastening to the shore or returning thence. The two walked, often separated but always finding each other again, in the middle of the street, without saying a word to each other, and were already traversing the suburb in which the guilds are domiciled. The disaster on the Brenta had aroused the whole population. Here were collected on every hand loudly talking or whispering groups, who gazed with sympathetic curiosity at the pair joined by the accident of a lost brother and bridegroom.

The monk and Diana were figures with which every child in Padua was acquainted. Astorre, though we cannot say that he was thought a saint, was at least reputed an exemplary monk. He might have been called the monk of the city of Padua, whom the people reverenced, and of whom they were proud. And with good reason; for bravely and joyfully he had renounced the privileges of his high birth and the incalculable riches of his family, in order, without counting the cost, in times of pestilence or other public calamity to hazard his life for the humblest man or the poorest woman. Moreover, with his curly brown hair, his comforting eyes, and his noble bearing, he was a man to whom all hearts were open, such a man as the people love in their saints.

Diana was in her way no less noted, if for no other reason, because of her robust form, which the common people admire more than delicate charms. Her mother was a German, indeed a Hohenstaufen, as some affirmed — only by blood, it is true, not according to law. Germany and Italy had like good sisters combined to produce this majestic figure.

Stern and austere as Diana was in association with her equals, she was gracious to the lowly, let them tell her of their affairs, gave terse and plain advice, and kissed the most ragged children. She bestowed and gave away without hesitation, probably because her father, old Pizzaguerra, next to Vicedomini the richest man in Padua, was at the same time the meanest niggard, and Diana was ashamed of her father's fault.

Accordingly, the devoted people in their hostelries and gossiping rooms gave her every month in marriage to some Paduan patrician; but reality took no account of these pious wishes. Three obstacles blocked the way to matrimony: Diana's elevated and often portentously gloomy eyebrows, her father's close fist, and the blind attachment of her brother Germano to the tyrant, in the case of whose possible fall the faithful servant could not but go to destruction too, dragging all his kin after him.

Finally, without love, as was a matter of common knowledge, she had been asked in marriage by Umberto Vicedomini, who now lay drowned in the Brenta.

For the rest, the two persons in question were so absorbed in their rightful grief that they either did not hear the eager chatter which followed close on their heels or did not concern themselves much with it. The occasion of this talk was not the fact that the monk and the woman were walking side by side. That seemed quite in order, since the monk had the duty of consoling her, and both, moreover, were presumably going the same way — to old Vicedomini's — as the most nearly affected and most natural reporters of the event.

The women were sorry for Diana, whose fate it had been to marry a man who had taken her only to fill the place

of a dear departed; and in the same breath they lamented
for her, that she had lost this man before the consummation of the wedlock.

The men, on the other hand, discussed with self-impor-
tant gesticulation and cunning mien a burning question
which had arisen on account of the drowning in the Brenta
of the four heirs relied upon to perpetuate the name of
the first family in Padua. The riches of the Vicedominis
were proverbial. The head of the family, a man as ener-
getic as he was crafty, who had contrived to keep on good
terms both with the five-times excommunicated tyrant of
Padua and with the church that had put him under its ban,
had never in all his days busied himself in the least with
public affairs, but had applied a tenacious life and magnificent powers of will to a single aim: the increase of the
wealth and prosperity of his family. Now this family was
annihilated. His eldest son and his grandsons lay in the
depths of the Brenta. The second and the third son had
in this very year of sorrow disappeared from off the face
of the earth, one of them two months, and the other three
months ago. The elder had been worn out in the service
of the tyrant and left behind on one of his wild battlefields.
The other, of whom the unprejudiced father had made a
great merchant in the Venetian style, had, on some strand
in the Orient, bled to death on a cross to which he had been
nailed by pirates, weary of waiting for delayed ransom.
As the fourth, there remained Astorre the monk. That
with the expenditure of his last ounce of strength he would
endeavor to extricate this fourth from the bondage of
monastic vows — of that, the shrewdly calculating Paduans
doubted not a moment. Whether he was destined to suc-
ceed, and whether the monk would lend himself to the
enterprise, was the question now debated up and down the
excited highway.

And the debate finally waxed so hot and vehement that
even the mourning monk could no longer remain in doubt
as to who were meant by the "he" and "she" that were

bandied about in the several groups. Therefore he turned, more for his companion's sake than for his own, into a shady, grass-grown street to which his sandaled foot was no stranger; for it led by the weather-beaten outer wall of his monastery. Here the air was cool even to chilliness; but the terrible news now broadcast over Padua had penetrated even these shadows. Through the open windows of the refectory that abutted upon the thick wall the conversation of the brothers at the belated noonday meal — the catastrophe on the Brenta had set awry all times and hours in the city — sounded so disputatious and uproarious, so full of *-inibus* and *-atibus* — for they talked in Latin or assailed each other with citations from the Decretals — that the monk readily divined that here too as on the street the same dilemma, or a similar one, was under discussion. And if he perhaps did not clearly determine of what, he knew to a certainty of whom the brothers were talking. One thing, however, which he did not discover —

Continuing all the while to speak, Dante sought out among his auditors the high-born cleric, who concealed himself behind his neighbor's back.

— was the fact that two gleaming hollow eyes were peering through a loophole in the wall at him and the woman by his side. These eyes belonged to a wretched creature, a forlorn monk by the name of Serapion, who was being consumed body and soul in the monastery. With his precipitate imagination he had immediately comprehended that his sworn brother Astorre had reached the end of his fasting and famishing according to the rule of St. Francis, and he madly envied him the possession of those worldly goods and joys which the caprice of death had allotted to him. He leered at the home-comer in order to scrutinize his features and in their expression to read what Astorre had resolved upon. His gaze devoured the woman and he followed her every footstep.

Astorre turned his steps and those of his sister-in-law to a little square formed by four castellated palaces, and with her entered the vaulted portal of the most splendid. On a stone bench in the court yard he caught sight of two recumbent figures, a boyish German clad in mail from head to foot and a hoary Saracen. The German, stretched out at full length in slumber, had laid his auburn curly head in the lap of the seated infidel who, likewise asleep, bent over him like a father with his snow-white beard. The pair belonged to Ezzelino's body-guard which, in imitation of his father-in-law's, the Emperor Frederick's, was composed of an equal number of Germans and Saracens. The tyrant was in the palace. He may have deemed it his duty to visit old Vicedomini. And in fact Astorre and Diana could hear, even from the winding stairway, what they were saying,—Ezzelino in brief and calm phrases, the old man, on the contrary, apparently quite beside himself, shouting and scolding at the top of his voice. The monk and the woman stopped at the door of the room in the midst of a pale group of domestics. The servants trembled in every limb. Their master had heaped the most violent imprecations upon them and had with clenched fists driven them out of his presence, because they had brought him belated news from the river-side and had hardly had the courage to stammer it forth. Moreover, this household had been petrified by the dreaded approach of the tyrant. On pain of death it was forbidden ever to announce his coming. Like an unheralded spirit he entered houses and apartments.

"And that, cruel monster, you relate as unconcernedly," the old man raved in his despair, " as though you were telling of the loss of a horse or a harvest. It is you who have killed the four, no one else than you! Why must you ride at that particular hour along the river? Why must you wave a greeting out upon the Brenta? You did it as an injury to me! Do you hear?"

" Fate," answered Ezzelino.

"Fate?" screamed Vicedomini. "Fate, and star-gazing, and conjurings, and conspiracies, and decapitations,— women casting themselves down from the roof to the pavement, and a hundred arrow-pierced youths falling from their horses in your infamous fool-hardy battles — that is the time and reign of Ezzelino, you accursed reprobate! All of us you drag in your bloody train, all life and death become violent and unnatural where your spirit rules, and no longer may any one await his end as a penitent Christian in his bed!"

"You do me wrong," replied the other. "For my part, I have indeed no dealings with the church. It does not concern me. But I have never hindered you and those like you from having to do with it. You know as much; otherwise you would never dare to carry on a correspondence with the Holy See. What are you twisting about there in your hands, concealing from me the papal seal? A letter of indulgence? A brief? Give it to me! In very truth, a brief! May I read it? Will you permit me? Your gracious benefactor, the Holy Father, writes you that in case your family should be reduced to your fourth and last son, the monk, he shall *ipso facto* be released from his vows, provided he return to the world of his own free will and accord. Sly fox, how many ounces of gold did this parchment cost you?"

"Do you hold me up to scorn?" roared the old man. "What else could I do after the death of my second and third sons? For whom should I have gathered and garnered? For the worms? For you? Do you mean to rob me? . . . No? Then help me, gossip,"— before his excommunication Ezzelino had been godfather to Vicedomini's third son, the one who had sacrificed himself for him on the battlefield — "help me prevail upon the monk to come back into the world and take a wife. Command him to do it, all-powerful prince. Give him to me to take the place of that son of mine whom you have slaughtered. Hold up my hands in this endeavor, if you love me!"

" That is no affair of mine," replied the tyrant, without the least concern. " Let him settle that with himself. ' Of his own free will and accord,' says the brief. Why, if he is a good monk, as I believe, should he change his state? In order that the blood of the Vicedominis shall not run dry? Is that a question of life and death for the world? Are the Vicedominis indispensable? "

Now the other howled in insensate fury, " You fiend! You murderer of my children! I see through your villainy! You wish to be my heir and carry on your cracked-brained campaigns with my money!" Then he perceived his daughter-in-law who, while the monk hesitated, had passed on through the group of servants and across the threshold. Despite his feebleness he plunged toward her with tottering steps, and seized and tugged at her hands, as though calling her to account for the calamity that had befallen them both. " What have you done with my son, Diana? " he panted.

" He lies in the Brenta," she answered sadly, and her blue eyes darkened.

" Where are my three grandsons? "

" In the Brenta," she repeated.

" And yourself you bring me as a gift? You I may keep? " The old man laughed discordantly.

" Would to God," she said slowly, " the waves were bearing me forth, and the others were standing here in my stead! "

She said no more. Then sudden anger seized her. " If the sight of me offends your eyes and you cannot bear my presence, then hold this man accountable. I was as good as dead; but he drew me by the hair out of the grave and restored me to life."

Not until now had the old man observed the monk, his son; and he collected himself with an energy and rapidity which the heavy grief seemed rather to have steeled than lamed.

" Really? He took you from the Brenta? Hm! Remarkable! The ways of God are indeed marvelous! "

He seized the monk by the arm and shoulder, as if to take possession of him, body and soul, and dragged him to his armchair, upon which he dropped, without releasing the compliant arm. Diana followed and kneeled on the other side of the chair, with folded hands, and laid her head upon the arm of the chair, so that only the knot of her blond hair remained visible, as though it were a lifeless object. Opposite the group sat Ezzelino, his right hand propped upon the roll of the brief, as though this were a field-marshal's baton.

" My boy, my boy," whimpered the old man with mingled tenderness of true affection and cunning, " my last and only comforter! You staff and stay of my old age will not break asunder in these trembling hands! . . . You understand," he continued in a dryer tone becoming at once matter-of-fact, " that as matters now stand there can be no question of your remaining in the monastery. The canon law itself provides — does it not, my son? — that a monk whose father becomes impoverished or falls sick shall be granted leave of absence by his prior to cultivate the family domain and support the author of his days. But I need you much more urgently. Your brothers and nephews are gone and you are now the only one to bear the torch which is the life of our house! You are a flame that I have kindled and it avails me nothing that it should flicker and consume itself in a cell. One thing let me tell you," — he had read unfeigned sympathy in the warm brown eyes, and the monk's reverent bearing seemed to promise blind obedience — " I am a sicker man than you think. Am I not, Issachar? " He turned backward toward an emaciated figure which, noiselessly entering by a side door, had come up behind the old man's chair with vial and spoon in his hands and now nodded his pale head in confirmation. " I go hence; but I tell you, Astorre, if you leave me deprived of my wish, your father will refuse to embark in the ferry of souls and will remain cowering on the gloomy strand!"

The monk tenderly stroked the old man's feverish hand, but answered with self-assurance, " My vows!"

Ezzelino unrolled the brief.

"Your vows?" said old Vicedomini ingratiatingly. "Loosened bonds! Parted fetters! Make a move and they will fall away. The holy church to which you owe veneration and obedience pronounces them null and void. Here it is in writing." His bony finger pointed to the parchment with the papal seal.

The monk humbly approached his sovereign, received the document, and read it, observed by two pairs of eyes. The letters swam before his vision and he reeled backward, as though, standing upon a high tower, he saw the railing suddenly give way.

Ezzelino came to the support of the staggerer with the brief question, " To whom did you make your vow, monk? To yourself, or to the church?"

" To both, of course," cried the old man in anger. " That is all cursèd hair-splitting. Be on your guard against that man, my son! He means to reduce us Vice-dominis to beggary."

Without resentment Ezzelino put his right hand upon his beard and swore, " When Vicedomini dies, the monk here, his son, shall be his heir, and — should the family become extinct with him, and he loves me and his native city — he shall found a hospital of a certain magnitude and magnificence, which will make the hundred cities " — he meant the cities of Italy — " envious of us. Now, gossip, since I have cleared myself of the reproach of rapacity, may I put a few more questions to the monk? Have I your permission?"

Then such a passion seized the old man that he fell into a paroxysm. But he did not yet let go the monk's arm, which he had again grasped.

Issachar cautiously held a spoonful of some strong-smelling essence up to the pale lips. With an effort the sufferer turned away his head. "Let me alone!" he groaned, "you are also physician to the Governor!" and closed his eyes.

The Jew turned his own eyes, which were lustrous black and very shrewd, upon the tyrant, as though beseeching pardon for this suspicion.

"Will he regain consciousness?" asked Ezzelino.

"I think so," answered the Jew. "He still lives and will awake again; but not for long, I fear. This day's sun he will not see at the setting."

The tyrant made use of the moment for a word with Astorre, who was busied with his unconscious father.

"Answer me, monk," said Ezzelino and — his favorite gesture — groped with the outstretched fingers of his right hand in his waving beard. "How much have the three vows cost you which, ten or more years ago — you are probably thirty?" — the monk nodded — "you solemnly took?"

Astorre opened wide his ingenuous eyes and replied without hesitation. "Poverty and obedience, nothing. I have no sense of proprietorship and I obey with ease." He paused and blushed.

The tyrant found something to admire in this masculine chastity. "Did this man here force your present state upon you, or wheedle you into it?" he asked, changing the subject.

"No," declared the monk. "Since time immemorial, as our genealogy relates, of every three or four sons in our house the last takes holy orders, whether in order that we Vicedominis may have an intercessor, or in order to keep intact the inheritance and the power of our house — no matter; the custom is ancient and venerable. I knew my lot, which was not repugnant to me, from early youth. No compulsion was put upon me."

"And the third?" Ezzelino resumed, meaning the third vow. Astorre understood him.

With a renewed blush, but this time a faint one, he replied, " It did not prove easy for me, but I have endured it as other monks have done, when they were well advised, as I was. By the blessed St. Anthony," he reverently added.

" This meritorious saint, as you know, my lords and ladies, dwelt for some years with the Franciscans in Padua," Dante explained.

" Why should we not know it? " jestingly remarked one of the listeners. " Forsooth, we have venerated the relic which swims around there in the convent pond — I mean the pike which whilom attended the homiletic ministrations of the saint, became converted, ate no more meat, was steadfast in well-doing, and even now, in his old age, as a strict vegetarian "— he swallowed the end of the farce; for Dante had frowned upon him.

"And what did he advise you to do? " asked Ezzelino.
" To take my state simply, rightly, and properly," the monk informed him, " as an exacting service, like military service, for instance, which also demands obedient muscles and imposes privations that a hardy soldier may not even feel to be such — to till the soil in the sweat of my brow, to eat moderately, to fast moderately, to hear confession from neither maidens nor young matrons, to walk humbly in the sight of God, and to adore his blessed Mother no more ardently than the breviary prescribes."
The tyrant smiled. Then he extended his right hand toward the monk, in admonition or blessing, and said, " Fortunate man! You have a lucky star! Your today grows easily out of your yesterday and imperceptibly becomes your tomorrow. You are something, and no slight thing either: for you fulfil the office of mercy, which I recognize, although I hold another office myself. Should you now enter the world, which obeys its own laws — laws that you are too old to learn — your bright star would be

transformed into a ridiculous will-o'-the-wisp and after
a few silly zig-zags would sputter its life out amid the
derision of the heavenly hosts.

" One thing more, and this I say as I have a right to
say it, as the ruler of Padua: your life was to my people
an edification, an example of renunciation. The poorest
man found comfort in it, seeing you share his frugal fare
and his daily toil. If you abandon the cowl and as a man
of rank woo a lady of rank, if with lavish hands you drain
the riches of your house, you will defraud the people, who
have adopted you as one of their own, you will make mal-
contents and insatiate busybodies in the state, and if
anger, disobedience, and insurrection should ensue, I should
not marvel. One cannot shake off the shackles of custom!

" Neither I nor Padua can spare you! Your handsome
and knightly figure strikes the eye of the multitude, and
you have more courage, or at least a nobler courage, than
your boorish brothers had. If the people, after their mad
fashion, are about to murder this man here " — he pointed
to Issachar — " because he brings them help — this was
indeed near to happening to the Jew during the last pestilence — who will defend him, as you did, against the raving
multitude, until I come and bid them halt ? "

" Issachar, help me persuade the monk! " said Ezzelino,
turning with a grim smile toward the physician. " For
your sake, if for no other reason, he must not discard the
cowl."

" My lord," lisped the latter, " under your sceptre the
foolish scene, which you punished no less justly than
bloodily, will hardly be repeated; and I, whose faith praises
the permanence of the family as God's supreme blessing,
would not be the cause wherefore His Illustrious Highness "
— by this title he already called the monk, no longer " His
Reverence "— " should remain unwed."

Ezzelino smiled at the Jew's subtlety. "And whither do
your thoughts tend, monk ? " he asked.

" They stand still and hold their ground! But I would—

God forgive me the sin — that my father might nevermore awake, and not compel me to be harsh with him! If he had only received the viaticum!" He impetuously kissed the patient's cheek, who thereat came back to consciousness.

Revived, Vicedomini breathed a deep sigh, raised his weary eyelids, and from under the gray tangle of his heavy eyebrows directed a look of entreaty at the monk. "How is it?" he asked. "What have you ordained for me, my best beloved, — heaven or hell?"

"Father," Astorre begged with a trembling voice, "your life has run its course. Your hour has come! Put away from you the thought of worldly goods and cares; think of the salvation of your soul! Behold, your priests" — he meant those of the parish church — "have gathered in the adjoining room and wait to bring you the most holy sacraments of the dying."

It was true. The door of the next room was silently opened and a feeble candle, hardly visible in the daylight, was seen glimmering, while a choir softly chanted and the gentle tinkling of a bell became audible.

At this moment the old man, who felt his knees already sinking beneath the cold waters of Lethe, clung fast to the monk, as of yore St. Peter to the Saviour on the lake of Gennesaret. "You will do it for me," he mumbled.

"If only I could! If I had the right!" sighed the monk. "By all the saints, father, I implore you, think of eternity! Forget the things of this earth! Your hour has come!"

This veiled refusal fanned the last spark of life in Vicedomini to a roaring flame. "Disobedient, ungrateful son!" he cried in anger.

Astorre beckoned to the priests.

"By all the devils of hell," raved the old man, "keep away from me with your rubbing and smearing! I have nothing to lose — I am a damned soul at best, and should remain one in the midst of the heavenly choir, if my son wantonly rebuffs me and spoils the seed of life that I have planted in him!"

The horrified monk, shuddering in the depths of his soul at this blood-curdling blasphemy, saw his father irrevocably consigned to eternal misery. So he thought and was thereof firmly persuaded, as in his place I too should have been. In dark despair he threw himself upon his knees before the dying man and amid a flood of tears implored him, "Sir, I adjure you, have mercy on yourself and on me!"

"Let the sly dog go his way," whispered the tyrant. The monk did not hear him.

Once more he signaled to the astounded priests, and the rites of the dying were about to begin.

But the old man doubled up like a stubborn child and shook his gray head.

"Let the schemer take his own course," Ezzelino admonished in a louder tone.

"Father, father!" sobbed the monk, and his soul was melted in pity.

"Illustrious lord and brother in Christ," a priest now asked in an uncertain voice, "are you duly prepared to receive the body of your Creator and Saviour?" The old man made no answer.

"Do you stand fast in faith in the Holy Trinity? Answer me, sir!" demanded the priest for the second time, and turned as white as a sheet; for with a strong voice the dying man cried, "Denied be it and cursed, cursed and—"

"No farther!" exclaimed the monk and sprang to his feet. "I am yours to command, sir. Do with me as you will. Only cast not yourself down into the flaming pit!"

The old man breathed a sigh, as if after making a great effort. Then, relieved, I had almost said contented, he gazed about him. With a groping hand he grasped the blond hair of Diana, drew the woman upward as she rose from her knees, took the hand which she did not refuse him, opened the clenched fist of the monk, and placed one within the other.

"Valid! Before the most holy sacrament!" he exulted,

and blessed the pair. The monk did not contradict, and Diana closed her eyes.

"Quickly now, reverend fathers!" the old man urged. "There is need of haste, as I think, and I am in a Christian disposition."

The monk and his betrothed started to withdraw behind the priestly band. "Remain!" murmured the dying man, "remain, that my comforted eyes may behold you together until the light goes out of them." Astorre and Diana, retreating no more than a few steps, were obliged to stand hand in hand within the expiring sight of the stubborn old man. He murmured a brief confession, received the Last Supper, and passed away, while they were anointing the soles of his feet and the priest was calling to his deaf ears that splendid farewell, "Go forth, Christian soul!" Even in death his face plainly wore the expression of triumphant craft.

While round about all were kneeling, the tyrant watched the sacred office seated and with calm attention, somewhat as one observes a strange custom, or as a scholar contemplates an ancient people depicted upon a sarcophagus in the act of making a sacrifice. He stepped up to the dead man and closed his eyes.

Then he turned to Diana. "Noble lady," he said, "I think we shall now do well to go home. Your parents, though informed of your rescue, are surely anxious to see you. Moreover, you are clad in a garb of lowliness which does not befit you."

"Prince, I thank you and will follow you," replied Diana. But she let her hand remain in the monk's, whose glance she had as yet avoided. Now she looked her husband full in the face and spoke with a deep but melodious voice, while her cheeks were suffused with purple, "My lord and master, it would not have been right for us to allow your father's soul to perish. So I became yours. Keep better faith with me than with the monastery. Your brother did not love me. Forgive me for saying it; I speak

the simple truth. You will have in me a good and obedient
wife. But I have two peculiarities of which you must be
careful. I am quick-tempered if my rights or my honor
are impugned, and over-nice in demanding that no promise
shall be made to me, unless it be kept. Even as a child I
hardly or not at all suffered promises to be broken. I have
few wishes and desire nothing beyond the ordinary; only,
when one has held something in prospect and given me
assurance of having it, then I need fulfilment of the promise; otherwise I lose confidence and am more deeply
wounded than other women by wrong. But by what right
do I speak thus to you, my lord and master, whom I hardly
know? Let me be silent. Farewell, my husband, and give
me nine days in which to mourn for your brother.'' Now
she slowly withdrew her hand from his and disappeared
with the tyrant.

Meanwhile the priestly band had removed the body, in
order to place it upon the bier in the private chapel and to
consecrate it.

Astorre stood alone in the monk's habit that he had forfeited and that covered a regretful breast. An army of
servants, who had witnessed and sufficiently comprehended
the strange scene, presented themselves in obsequious
attitudes and with gestures of timidity to their new master,
amazed and intimidated less by the change of employer
than by the supposed sacrilege of the broken vows — the
brief had been read in too low a tone for them to hear its
purport — and the secularization of the reverend monk.
Astorre could not bring himself to mourn for his father.
There crept over him, now that he had regained self-con-
trol, the suspicion — let me rather say the revolting certainty overwhelmed him that a dying man had abused his
confidence and taken unfair advantage of his pity. He
discovered in the old man's despair of salvation the lurk-
ing-place of craft, and in his wild blasphemy a calculated
game of chance on the threshold of death. Angrily, almost
malevolently his thoughts turned to the woman who had

fallen to his lot. The fantastic monkish idea tempted him, to love her not with his own heart but only as the representative of his departed brother; but his sound sense and his native honesty rejected this shameful subterfuge. Regarding her now as his own, he could not repel a certain wonderment that his wife had confronted him with such plain speech and blunt sincerity, and had so dispassionately sought an understanding with him, without veil or cover — a much more real and tangible figure than the airy creatures of the legends. He had thought women were made of softer clay.

Now the monk suddenly became aware of the cloak of his order and the contradiction which it presented to his feelings and the trend of his thoughts. His cowl put him to shame and weighed heavily upon him. " Give me worldly garments," he commanded. Assiduous servants surrounded him, from whose midst he soon stepped forth clad in the garb of his drowned brother, with whom he was of about equal size.

At the same moment his father's jester, Gocciola by name, kneeled at his feet and paid him homage, not, like the others, to plead for retention in his service, but begging discharge and permission to change his condition; for he was weary of the world, he said, his hair was growing gray, and it would ill become him to wear his cap and jingling bells on the journey to the great beyond. With these querulous words he took possession of the discarded cowl, which the servants had dared not touch. But his muddled brain turned topsy-turvy and he added greedily, " I should like to have some *amarelle* to eat once more before I say farewell to the world and its delusions! There will not be long to wait for a wedding here, I think." He licked the corners of his mouth with his coated tongue. Then he bent a knee before the monk, shook his bells, and darted away, dragging the cowl after him.

"*Amarelle* or *amare*," Dante explained, " is the wedding cake of Padua, so called because of its bitter almond-flavor and at the same time with a graceful allusion to the verb of the first conjugation.'' Here the narrator paused and shaded his brow and eyes with his hand, meditating upon the further course of his story.

Meanwhile the prince's major-domo, an Alsatian named Burkhard, walked in with measured steps, ceremonious bows, and circumstantial excuses for having to interrupt the conversation, presented himself to Cangrande, and asked for instructions concerning some domestic matter. Germans were at that time not infrequently found at the Ghibelline courts of Italy,—indeed, they were in demand, and were preferred to the natives on account of their probity and their instinct for ceremonies and usages.

When Dante again raised his head he caught sight of the Alsatian and heard his Italian, which persistently confounded soft and hard consonants, to the amusement of the court but to the excruciating torture of the poet's sensitive ear. His glance then lingered with visible pleasure upon the two youths, Ascanio and the mailed warrior. Finally, he allowed it to rest meditatively upon the two ladies, the princess Diana, who had become more animated and whose marble cheek had flushed slightly, and upon Antiope, Cangrande's friend, a pretty and ingenuous girl. Then he continued:

Behind the palace of the Vicedominis there formerly extended — now that the illustrious family is long since extinct that place has completely changed — a spacious estate down to the foot of the broad, fortified city wall, so spacious that it contained pasturage for herds, preserves for deer, ponds stocked with fish, dense shady woods and sunlit grape-arbors. On a glorious morning a week after the funeral Astorre the monk — for during his brief earthly career he kept this name among the Paduans, in spite of the fact of his secularization — Astorre, I say, sat in the dark shade of a cedar, leaning against the trunk and stretching the tips of his shoes out into the burning sunlight. He was sitting or lying in front of a fountain that threw out a cool stream from the mouth of an indifferent mask, not far from a stone bench, which he did not occupy because of preference for the soft cushion of the luxuriant turf.

While he was thinking or dreaming, I know not of what, two young men, one in armor, the other daintily clad, though in traveling costume, dismounted from their dust-stained horses on the square in front of the palace, then almost entirely under the glare of the mid-day sun. Ascanio and Germano, as the horsemen were called, were the favorites of the Governor and had been youthful play-mates of the monk, with whom as with brothers he had studied and disported himself up to his fifteenth year, the beginning of his novitiate. Ezzelino had sent them as mes-sengers to his father-in-law, Emperor Frederick.

Dante paused and bowed at the mention of that great name.

With answers to their messages the two were returning to the tyrant, to whom, moreover, they were bringing the news of the day: a copy, made in the Imperial Chancery, of the pastoral letter addressed to the Christian clergy, in which, before the eyes of the whole world, the Holy Father accuses the witty emperor of extreme godlessness.

Although intrusted with weighty, perhaps urgent com-missions and with this portentous document, the two young men could not bring themselves to gallop past their old playmate's home directly to the tyrant's palace. In their last baiting-place before reaching Padua where, without taking their feet from the stirrups, they had had their horses fed and watered, the talkative landlord had told them of the great public misfortune and the still greater public scandal, the drowning of the wedding party and the monk's throwing off of his cowl, with pretty much all the circumstances, save Diana's and Astorre's joining of hands, which had not yet become generally known. Im-perishable the ties that bind us to the playmates of our childhood! Appalled by the strange fate of Astorre, the two could not rest until with their own eyes they had seen him, the friend restored to them. For long years they had no more than met the monk, by chance on the street, greeting him with a nod, friendly indeed, but abashed by sincere reverence, and somewhat distant.

Gocciola, whom they had found in the palace courtyard, dangling his feet from a wall and munching a roll, led them into the garden. Strolling along ahead of the youths, the fool regaled them not with the tragic fate of the house, but with his own affairs, which seemed to him by far the more important matter. He related that he ardently longed for a blissful end, and in the course of his confession swallowed the rest of the roll without having taken it between his loose teeth, so that it nearly strangled him. At the faces that he made and at his longing for a cell in the monastery Ascanio burst out laughing so merrily that he would have driven the clouds from the sky if on this day the sky had not with its own joy beamed resplendently.

Ascanio could not refrain from bantering the wretch, if only to get rid of his undesirable company. "Poor old fellow," he began, "you will never see the inside of a cell; for, between ourselves, in the strictest confidence, my uncle the tyrant has cast envious glances at you. Let me tell you that he has four fools, the Stoic, the Epicurean, the Platonist, and the Skeptic, as he calls them. When his grave highness wishes to jest, the four take their places at a signal from him in the four corners of the hall, the vaulted ceiling of which is adorned with the starry heavens and the revolving planets. My uncle, in informal dress, steps into the middle of the room, claps his hands, and with a hop and skip the philosophers change corners. Day before yesterday the Stoic whined and howled his life out because, glutton that he was, he had devoured many pounds of noodles at a sitting. My uncle has intimated to me that he intends to replace him, and to ask for you, Gocciola, as an inheritance tax from the monk, your new master. That is the way matters stand. Ezzelino is after you. Who knows but that he is now at your heels?" This was an allusion to the omnipresence of the tyrant, which kept the Paduans in constant fear and trembling. Gocciola uttered an outcry, as if the hand of the man of might were descending upon his shoulder, looked about, and, though nothing was following him but his abbreviated shadow, fled with chattering teeth to some convenient hiding-place.

"I will strike out Ezzelino's fools," Dante interrupted his narrative to say, and made a motion like the stroke of a pen, as though he were writing his story instead of telling it, as he was. "This trait is not true, or, if it is a part of my matter, Ascanio was lying. It is quite inconceivable that a mind so serious and naturally so noble as Ezzelino's should have kept fools and taken pleasure in their idiocy." This was a home thrust directed by the Florentine at his host, upon whose mantle Gocciola sat, grinning at the poet.

Cangrande did nothing of the sort. He made a secret vow to pay back Dante with interest at the first opportunity.

Satisfied, almost cheerful, Dante continued his narrative:

Finally the pair discovered the unfrocked monk leaning, as I have said, against a pine tree —

"Against a cedar, Dante," the princess, now become attentive, corrected him.

— a cedar, and sunning his toes. He did not notice those approaching him on either side, so absorbed was he in his vain or thoughtful dreaming. Now the mischievous Ascanio bent over to get a spear of grass, broke it off, and tickled the monk's nose, so that he sneezed loudly three times. Astorre cordially grasped the hands of his former playmates and drew them down upon the turf beside him, one to the right and the other to the left. "Well, what do you say of it?" he asked, in a tone more timid than challenging.

" First let me frankly praise your prior and your monastery ! " said Ascanio in fun. " They have kept you in good shape. You look younger than either of us. To be sure, the close-fitting worldly garb and your smooth chin may have their rejuvenating effect. Do you know that you are a handsome man? You are lying here under your giant cedar like the first man, whom, as scholars affirm, God created a man of thirty, and I," he continued with an expression of innocence, seeing that the monk blushed at his wantonness, " I am really the last to blame you for having escaped from the cowl; for to perpetuate its kind is the wish of every living thing."

" It was not my wish nor free resolve," the monk truthfully confessed. " With reluctance I did the will of my dying father."

" Really? " smiled Ascanio. " Tell that, Astorre, to no one but us, who love you. In the eyes of others this lack of independence would make you seem ridiculous or even contemptible. And now that we are talking of the ridiculous, take care, I beg you, Astorre, to develop the man out of the monk without offending against good taste! The ticklish transit must be very discreetly guarded and graduated. Take my advice and travel for a year,— to the Emperor's court, for example, whence to Padua and back couriers are incessantly running. Get Ezzelino to send you to Palermo! There, besides the most perfect knight and the most unprejudiced human being — I mean our Frederick the Second — you will make some acquaintance with women, and will break off the monkish habit of either deifying or contemning them. The spirit of the ruler gives its color to court and city . Wild, immoderate, and impetuous as life has become here in Padua under my uncle the tyrant, it gives you a false picture of the world. Palermo, where under the most humane of monarchs, jest and seriousness, virtue and pleasure, fidelity and inconstancy, simple faith and wise distrust are mingled in the right proportions — Palermo offers the truer picture. There for a year you may dance attendance upon the ladies, friends or foes, in permissible or pardonable fashion "— the monk frowned —" you will perhaps take part in a campaign or two, without however incautiously exposing yourself — remember your destiny — merely to remind yourself how to handle a horse and a sword — as a boy you knew! — you keep your jolly brown eyes open to everything in sight — by the torch of Aurora, how they flash and sparkle since you quit the monastery! — and you will return to us as a man who has himself in hand and others at his command."

" There at the Emperor's he must marry a Suabian," good-naturedly advised the youth in armor. " They are more dutiful and more reliable than our women."

" Will you stop talking? " Ascanio admonished him with a threatening finger. " No more of your straw-colored braids for me! " But the monk pressed Germano's right hand, which he had not yet released.

" Honestly, Germano, what do you think of it? "

" Of what? " he asked bluntly.

" Why, of my new state."

" Astorre, my friend," responded the moustachioed warrior somewhat embarrassed, " when a thing has been done, we do not go around asking for advice. We stand our ground. But if you insist upon knowing my opinion, why, you see, Astorre, disloyalty, broken promises, desertion, and so forth, those are all given hard names in Germany. Of course, your case is quite different, there is no comparison — and then, your dying father! Astorre, my dear friend, you acted handsomely; but the opposite would have been handsomer. That is my opinion," he frankly concluded.

" Then, Germano, if you had been present you would have refused me your sister's hand? "

That was a bolt out of a clear sky. " My sister's hand? Diana's, who is in mourning for your brother? "

" Diana's. She is my betrothed."

"Oh, magnificent!" cried now the worldly-wise Ascanio; and with "Delightful!" Germano chimed in. "Embrace me, brother-in-law." Notwithstanding his directness the soldier had good manners. But he suppressed a sigh. Dearly as he loved and esteemed his austere sister, he would, according to his natural feeling, have given the monk now sitting beside him a different wife.

So he twirled his moustache and Ascanio steered the conversation in a new direction. "Really, Astorre," chatted the gay fellow, "we must begin by getting acquainted all over again. Nothing less than those fifteen contemplative monastic years of yours lies between our childhood and today. Not that meanwhile we have changed our natures — who ever does that? — but that we have grown to the full stature of our manhood. This fellow, for instance," — he pointed to Germano — "now enjoys a fine military reputation; but I have to complain that he has become half a German. He" — Ascanio crooked his arm, as though he were draining a goblet — "and after that he grows melancholy and quarrelsome. Moreover, he despises our sweet Italian tongue. 'I will talk German with you!' he boasts, and growls forth the ursine tones of an inhuman speech. Then his servants grow pale, his creditors flee, and our Paduan ladies turn their stately backs upon him. Consequently, he has perhaps remained as chaste as you, Astorre." And he laid his hand confidingly upon the monk's shoulder.

Germano laughed heartily and retorted, pointing to Ascanio, "And this fellow here has fulfilled his destiny by becoming a perfect courtier."

"In that, you are wrong, Germano," Ezzelino's favorite contradicted him. "My destiny was to take life easily and to enjoy it with a cheerful heart." And by way of proof of this assertion he summoned with an amiable command the gardener's daughter whom he saw stealing by at a little distance and looking out of the corner of her eye at her new master, the monk. Laughing the while, the pretty creature was carrying on her head a basket filled to overflowing with grapes and figs, and looked rather roguish than bashful. Ascanio had jumped to his feet. He put his left arm about the girl's slender waist and with his right hand helped himself to a bunch of grapes from the basket. At the same time he sought a taste of the ripe lips. " I am thirsty," he said. The maiden acted shamefacedly but stood still, because she did not wish to spill her fruit. Disapproving this frivolity, the monk turned away from the pair, and the startled little hussy hastily fled at sight of the severe monkish reproof, strewing her path with tumbling fruit. Ascanio, who had kept his grapes in his hand, picked up two other bunches from the trail of the fugitive, one of which he offered to Germano; but he contemptuously threw the unpressed grapes into the grass. The other bunch the mischief-maker passed to the monk, who likewise left them untouched for a while, but then without thinking tasted one juicy grape, and soon a second, and a third.

"A courtier?" Ascanio continued, who, amused at the daintiness of the monk of thirty, had again dropped upon the turf beside him. " Do not believe that, Astorre. Believe the contrary. I am the only one to urge my uncle, gently but in a way that he can understand, not to grow merciless, to remain a man."

" He is no more than just and true to himself," said Germano.

"A fig for his justice!" cried Ascanio. "And for his logic! Padua is a fief of the empire. Ezzelino is the Governor. Whoever incurs his displeasure is a rebel against the empire. Those guilty of high treason—" He could not bring himself to utter the word. " Horrible!" he murmured. "And in any event, why are we Italians not suffered to live our own lives under the warm rays of our own sun? Why this cloud of a phantom empire to take our breath away? I do not speak for myself. I am bound to my uncle. If the Emperor—whom God preserve—

should die, all Italy will fall with curses and execrations upon the tyrant Ezzelino, and they will just strangle his nephew in passing." Ascanio surveyed the radiant sky above this fertile earth and heaved a sigh.

"Both of us," Germano coolly added. "But there is time enough for that. The Governor has obtained a definite prediction. The learned Guido Bonatti and Paul of Bagdad, whose long beard sweeps the dust on the street, have with one accord, despite their mutual jealousy and their habit of mutual contradiction, read the riddle of a new and strange constellation as follows: sooner or later a son of the Peninsula will gain its undivided crown, with the help of a German emperor who for his part will roll together on the other side of the mountains everything German into a single hard ball, the apple of the empire. Is Frederick this emperor? Is Ezzelino this king? God knows; for He knows the time and the hour; but the Governor has staked his fame and our heads on this consummation."

"Whimsy, woven of sense and folly!" ejaculated Ascanio, while the monk marveled at the potent influence of the stars, the far-reaching ambition of rulers, and the irresistible current of the stream of life. Terrible also was the spectre of cruelty drawing ever nearer in the deeds of Ezzelino, whom the innocent monk had revered as justice personified.

Ascanio answered his unuttered queries by continuing, "May they both come to an evil end, the scowling Guido and the bearded heathen! They beguile my uncle into yielding to his whims and lusts in the belief that he is doing only what necessity demands. Have you ever seen, Germano, how at his frugal meal he colors the water in his transparent crystal goblet with the three or four drops of blood-red Sicilian wine that he allows himself? How his attentive eye follows the blood as it slowly unfolds like a cloud and spreads through the clear water? Or how he likes to close the eyes of the dead, so that it has almost become an obligation of courtesy to invite the Governor

to deathbeds as to a festival, and to leave this sad office
to him? Ezzelino, my Prince, I adjure you, do not become
cruel!'' cried the youth, overwhelmed by his feelings.

''I think not, nephew,'' said a voice behind him. It was
Ezzelino, who had drawn near unobserved and, though not
an eavesdropper, had heard Ascanio's last painful outcry.

The three youths rose quickly and greeted the ruler, who
seated himself upon the bench. His face was as imper-
turbable as the mask of the fountain.

''My messengers,'' he demanded of Ascanio and Germano, ''what possessed you to visit this man here ''—he
nodded slightly in the direction of the monk—''before
reporting to me?''

''He is the playmate of our youth and has had strange
experiences,'' the nephew gave as his excuse, and Ezzelino
let it pass. He took the letters which on bended knee
Ascanio delivered to him. He thrust all into his bosom
except the papal bull. ''Behold,'' said he, ''the latest
news! Read it to me, Ascanio. Your eyes are better than
mine.''

Ascanio read the apostolic epistle aloud while Ezzelino
buried his right hand in his beard and listened with demonic glee.

At the beginning the triple-crowned author gave the
witty Emperor the name of an Apocalyptic beast. ''You
need not tell me that; it is absurd,'' said the tyrant. ''In
his letters the pontifex also gave me extravagant titles
until I admonished him to chide me, who am called Ezzelino
the Roman, henceforth in a classical language. What does
he call me this time, I wonder? Find the place, Ascanio,—
there must be one—where he reproves my father-in-law
for his evil associations. Give it here!'' He seized the
document and soon found the passage. Here the pope
accused the Emperor of loving his daughter's husband,
''Ezzelino da Romano, the greatest criminal on the in-
habited earth.''

''Correct!'' was Ezzelino's approving comment as he

returned the document to Ascanio. "Read to me about the Emperor's godless deeds, nephew," he smiled.

Ascanio read to the effect that Frederick had said there were, besides many fictions of diseased brains, only two true gods, nature and reason. The tyrant shrugged his shoulders.

Ascanio read on: Frederick had declared that three mountebanks, Moses, Mohammed, and — he held his breath — had imposed upon the world. "Superficial," Ezzelino objected, "they followed their stars and each had his day; but spoken or not, that sentence will sink in and is equivalent to an army and a fleet for him who wears the tiara. Proceed."

A weird tale came next in order. Riding through a field of waving grain Frederick was reported to have jested with his followers and in blasphemous allusion to the holy sacrament of the mass to have regaled them with this triplet:

> There are gods as many as ears that grow
> On the cornstalks ranged in a sunny row,
> All nodding their heads when the breezes blow —

Ezzelino bethought himself. "Strange," he whispered. "My memory has retained these verses. They are quite authentic. The Emperor with a merry laugh called them out to me when, face to face with the ruined temples of Enna, we rode together through those teeming cornfields with which the goddess Ceres has blessed the Sicilian soil. My recollection is as clear as the sunlight which on that summer day illumined the island. It was not I who reported this merry jest to the pontiff. I am too serious for that. Who did it? I will let you be the judges, young men. We were a trio of riders, and the third — of this also I am as certain as of yonder luminous sun " — at that moment a ray pierced the foliage — " was Pietro della Vigna, the Emperor's inseparable companion. Can the pious chancellor have trembled for his soul and have eased his conscience by writing a letter to Rome? Does a Saracen messenger ride today? Yes? Then quickly, Ascanio, I will dictate a line."

Ascanio took out his tablet and pencil, dropped upon his right knee, using his left as a support for the tablet, and wrote:

"Exalted master and dear father! A word in haste. The verses in the papal bull—you are too clever to repeat yourself—only two pairs of ears ever heard, mine and those of your Pietro in the cornfields of Enna a year ago, when you summoned me to your court and with you I traversed the island. No cock will ever crow because of them, unless it be the one in the gospel that confirmed the treachery of Peter. If you love me and love your own life, my lord, put your chancellor to the test of a sharp question."

"Bloody play on the name! I will not write that. My hand trembles," cried Ascanio, turning pale. "I will not put the chancellor on the rack!" And he threw down the pencil.

"Official business," remarked Germano dryly, picked up the pencil and finished the letter, putting it under his helmet. "It shall be dispatched today. The Capuan is not to my simple mind, and never has been; he has an inscrutable countenance."

The monk Astorre shivered in spite of the mid-day sun. For the first time, he who had left the tranquil cloister saw and comprehended, as though he held it like the slippery coils of an adder in his own hand, the suspicion or the treachery of the world. From his brooding he was aroused by a stern word which Ezzelino, rising from his stone bench, addressed to him.

"Say, monk, why do you bury yourself in your house? You have not once left it since you donned secular garb. You fear public opinion? Meet it squarely! It will retreat before you. But if you make a move to flee, it will cling to your heels like a howling pack. Have you visited Diana, your betrothed? The week of mourning is past. Take my advice: this very day invite your kindred, and this very day make Diana your wife!"

"And then away with you to your farthest castle!" said Ascanio in conclusion.

"That I do not advise," the tyrant overruled him. "No fright. No flight. Today you wed and tomorrow you celebrate the wedding with music and a masquerade. Farewell." He departed, with a sign to Germano to follow him.

"May I interrupt?" asked Cangrande, who had been polite enough to await a natural pause in the narrative.

"You are the master," rejoined the Florentine briefly.

"Do you believe the immortal Emperor made that remark about the three great mountebanks?"

"*Non liquet.*"

"I mean, in your secret soul."

Dante shook his head in plain denial.

"And yet you have condemned him as one of the godless to the sixth circle of your hell. By what right did you that? Justify yourself!"

"Magnificence," answered the Florentine, "my Comedy addresses itself to my age. But this age rightly or wrongly reads the most frightful blasphemies in the lines of that sublime brow. I am powerless to oppose the pious opinion. The future will perhaps judge differently."

"My Dante," asked Cangrande for the second time, "do you believe Pietro della Vigna innocent of high treason?"

"*Non liquet.*"

"I mean, in your secret soul."

Dante repeated his gesture of denial.

"And in your Comedy you let the traitor avow his innocence?"

"My lord," the Florentine justified himself, "in the lack of clear proofs shall I accuse of treason one more son of the Peninsula, seeing that so many plotters and dissemblers go about among us?"

"Dante, my Dante," said the prince, "you believe innocent and you condemn! You believe guilty and you ac-
quit!" Then in a playful mood he continued the story:
"The monk and Ascanio also left the garden and entered
the hall." But Dante silenced him.

By no means. On the contrary, they mounted to a tower
room, the very one that Astorre as a curly-headed boy had
occupied; for he avoided the pretentious great apartments
which he must yet accustom himself to regard as his, in the
same way that he had avoided touching even with the tip
of his finger the golden hoard that he had inherited. Following the two came, obedient to a mute command of
Ascanio's, Burkhard, the major-domo, at a proper distance,
walking stiffly and displaying vexation in every mien.

Cangrande's master of ceremonies who bore the same
name had dispatched his business and returned intently
curious to the hall; for he had perceived that there was
a question of well-known persons. Hearing now his own
name mentioned, and seeing himself without warning reflected life-size in the mirror of the tale, he found this
liberty taken with his honorable person bold and altogether
unseemly on the part of the fugitive scholar whom they
suffered to abide with them for a season and to whom, in
just consideration of circumstances and proper distinctions,
he had assigned the plainest room conceivable in the upper
story of the princely residence. What the others had smilingly endured he felt as an abomination. He frowned and
rolled his eyes. The Florentine amused himself in all
seriousness at the indignation of the pedant and refused
to be disturbed in the continuation of his story.

"Worthy sir," Ascanio asked the major-domo—have I
said that he was an Alsatian by birth?—"how are marriages performed in Padua? Astorre and I are inexperienced children in respect to this science."

The master of ceremonies struck an attitude, looking fixedly at his lord, without paying the slightest attention to Ascanio who, according to his ideas, had no authority over him.

" *Distinguendum est*," he said solemnly. " There must be no confusion between asking in marriage, wedding, and nuptial celebration."

" Where is that written? " asked Ascanio in mock seriousness.

" *Ecce!* " answered the major-domo, unwrapping a great book which he carried constantly with him. " Here! " — pointing with the extended finger of his left hand to the title, which ran, " The Ceremonies of Padua, compiled from strict Investigation for the Use and Profit of Honorable and Polite Society, by Messer Godoscalco Burcardo." He turned the leaves and read, " Part I: Asking in Marriage. Paragraph I: The earnest suitor is accompanied by a friend of equal rank, as a competent witness — "

" By the superfluous merits of my patron saint," Ascanio interrupted him impatiently, " a truce with your *ante* and *post*, your asking in marriage and nuptials; serve us the meat of the matter: how are marriages performed in Padua? "

" In Batua," croaked the irritated Alsatian, whose barbarous accent was in his perturbation of spirits even more noticeable than usually, " the ten first families " — he enumerated them from memory — " are invited to esbousals among the nobility ten days in advance, neither sooner nor later, by the major-domo of the bridegroom at the head of six servants. In this illustrious assembly the rings are given and taken. Cybrian wine is served and for wedding cake *amarelle* — "

" God grant we may lose no teeth eating them! " laughed Ascanio; and snatching the book from the major-domo, he ran through the names, of which six heads of families — six out of twelve — and several young men had been stricken out with broad strokes of a pencil. They had presumably become involved in some conspiracy against the tyrant and had perished in consequence.

"Attention, old man!" Ascanio commanded, acting for the monk, who had sunk back into an armchair and, lost in thought, made no objection to his friend's assumption of authority. "You make your rounds with the six sluggards this minute, immediately, without delay, do you understand? And you will convey an invitation for today at the hour of vespers."

"Ten days in advance," repeated Herr Burkhard majestically, as though he were promulgating a law of the Empire.

"Today and for today, bull-head!"

"Impossible," said the major-domo calmly. "Will you alter the course of the stars and seasons?"

"Do you rebel? Is your neck itching for the ax, old man?" Ascanio warned him with a peculiar smile.

That sufficed. Herr Burkhard guessed the meaning. Ezzelino had given the command and the most stubborn of formalists yielded without a murmur, knowing that the tyrant ruled with a rod of iron.

"So you will not invite the two Ladies Canossa, Olympia and Antiope?"

"Why not invite them?" asked the monk suddenly, as if touched by a magic wand. The light of his eyes became tinged with color and a vision took form, the bare outline of which captivated his soul.

"Because Countess Olympia is out of her head, Astorre. Do you not know the poor woman's story? But, of course, you were then in your swaddling clothes — I mean in your cowl. It was three years ago, when the leaves were beginning to turn."

"In the summer, Ascanio, just three years ago," contradicted the monk.

"You are right — do you know the story after all? But how should you? At that time Count Canossa conferred privily with the papal legate, was detected, seized, and condemned. The Countess prostrated herself before my uncle, who retreated behind the veil of his silence. She was then most criminally deceived by a covetous chamberlain who, to gain money, deluded her with the expectation that the Count would be pardoned at the block. This expectation was not fulfilled and when they brought home to the Countess her husband beheaded, she, hurled thus headlong from hope to despair, cast herself out of the window down to where he was — marvelous to relate, without injury, except that she sprained her ankle. But from that day on her mind was unbalanced. Whereas natural moods blend imperceptibly one into another, as expiring daylight into the growing dusk, her moods change in furious rotation a dozen times in as many hours. Goaded by constant restlessness, the wretched woman rushes from her desolate city palace to her country estate, and thence back to the city in endless wandering. Today she is determined to marry her daughter to the son of a tenant, because lowliness alone can guarantee protection and peace; tomorrow the noblest suitor — who, by the way, for fear of such a mother, fails to present himself — would hardly be high-born enough — ''

If Ascanio, during this flood of eloquence, had cast the most fleeting glance at the monk, he would have stopped in amazement; for the monk's face was transfigured with pity and compassion.

'' When the tyrant,'' continued the unobserving narrator, '' rides past Olympia's dwelling on his way to the hunt, she rushes to the window and expects that, dismounting before her door, he will conduct her, as one who has incurred his displeasure but has now been tried with tribulation enough, mercifully and graciously back to his court — whereto, verily, he has no inclination. Another day, or even on the same day, she imagines herself persecuted and banished by Ezzelino, who does not bother himself with her. She believes herself impoverished and believes her

goods confiscated, which he has left untouched. Thus she
suffers the hot and cold fits of the most violent contrasts,
not only is herself distraught, but distracts all whom she
draws into the eddy of her giddy mind and — being only
half mad, she often speaks with precision and wit — she
does mischief wherever people believe her. There can be
no thought of inviting her to a social gathering and to a
festival. It is a miracle that her daughter Antiope, whom
she adores and whose marriage revolves about the centre
of her cyclonic fantasies, keeps her wits with only this tottering ground to stand on. But the girl, who is in the first
bloom of youth and is tolerably good-looking, has a healthy
nature. . . ." So he went on for some time yet.

But Astorre became absorbed in his dream. I say this,
because past events are a dream. For the monk saw what
he had witnessed three years before — a block, the headsman beside it, and himself, representing a sick clerical
brother, as the comforter awaiting a poor sinner condemned
to death. This man — Count Canossa — was brought in
fetters, but would not on any account yield, either because,
standing before the block, he trusted that his reprieve
would not longer be delayed, or simply because he loved
the sunlight and abhorred the grave. He rebuffed the
monk and disdained his prayers. A terrible struggle was
imminent if he continued his dogged resistance; for he
held his child by the hand, who — unobserved by the guards
— had run to embrace him, fastening the most expressive
and most entreating eyes upon the monk. The father
clasped the girl to his breast and seemingly wished by
means of this young life to protect himself from destruction, but was forced by the executioner to kneel and place
his head upon the block. Then the child laid her head and
neck beside her father's. Did she wish to stir the headsman to pity? Did she wish to encourage her father to
suffer the inevitable? Did she wish to breathe the name
of a saint into the ear that would not hear? Did she do

the unheard-of deed without reflection and forethought, from sheer excess of filial affection? Did she simply wish to die with him?

Now the colors shone so brightly that the monk saw in perfect lifelikeness only a few paces away the two necks lying side by side, the ruddy neck of the Count and the snow-white one of the child, with its ringlets of golden hair. This neck was most beautiful in form and of uncommon delicacy. Astorre trembled lest the falling ax might err, and he shuddered now in his inmost soul, not otherwise than the first time, save that his senses did not leave him as they had done when the frightful scene took place in reality before his eyes and he regained consciousness only when all was over.

"Has my lord and master any commission to give me?" Astorre was aroused from his trance by the rasping voice of the major-domo who was restive under Ascanio's assumed authority.

"Burcardo," replied Astorre in soft accents, "do not forget to invite the two Ladies Canossa, mother and daughter. Let it not be said that the monk holds himself aloof from those who are shunned and forsaken by the world. I respect the right of an unfortunate woman"—to this the major-domo eagerly nodded assent—"to be invited and to be received here. Should we pass her by, she might be deeply wounded, being as she is."

"Not for the world!" cried Ascanio in warning. "Do not subject yourself to *that* injury! Your betrothal itself is fantastic enough! And the fantastic inspires lunatics with enthusiasm. As is her way, she will do some incredible thing and launch some mad speech in the midst of the festivity, which is already sufficiently exciting to the women of Padua."

Herr Burkhard, however, who with bull-dog tenacity clung to the right of a Canossa, sane or insane, to join in every assembly of the twelve, and who believed himself bound to obey Vicedomini and no other, bowed low before the monk. "Your lordship alone shall be obeyed," he said and departed.

"O monk, monk," cried Ascanio, "you bring pity into a world in which goodness itself is hardly suffered to go unpunished!"

"But we men being as we are," Dante interpolated, "a prophetic light often reveals to us the edge of an abyss; then, however, wit comes, and argues, and smiles, and makes us believe that there is no danger.

So the shallow courtier first questioned and then reassured himself, saying, What earthly connection is there between the crazy woman and the monk, in whose life she does not play the least part? And after all, if she provokes mirth, she will give spice to the *amarelle!* He had not the remotest premonition of what was passing in Astorre's mind; but even though he had guessed and queried, the monk would not have abandoned his chaste secret to the worldling.

Accordingly Ascanio let the matter rest, and remembering the other command of the tyrant, to get the monk out among people, he asked merrily, "Have you procured the wedding ring, Astorre? For it is written in the Ceremonies, Part II, Paragraph so-and-so, 'There is an exchange of rings.'" The monk replied that something of the sort would probably be found among the family treasures.

"Not so, Astorre," said Ascanio. "If you take my advice, you will buy your Diana a new one. Who knows what memories cling to rings that have once been used? Turn your back upon ancient history. Moreover, it happens most charmingly — you can buy her a ring of the Florentine on the bridge. Do you know the man? But how should you? Listen! Early this morning when I was returning to town with Germano and started to cross our only bridge over the canal — we had to dismount and lead our horses, so dense was the throng — faith, on the weatherworn coping of the pier a goldsmith had opened shop and all Padua was rummaging among his wares and bargaining with him. Why upon the narrow bridge, Astorre, when we have so many public squares? Because in Florence the jewelers' shops are situated on the bridge over the Arno. For — wondrous is the logic of fashion! — of whom is jewelry bought if not of a Florentine, and where does a Florentine display his wares if not on a bridge? It is not done otherwise. Elsewhere his wares would be crude trumpery and he himself no true Florentine. But this man, I judge, is a Florentine. Indeed, over his booth he has written in gigantic letters, *Niccolò Lippo dei Lippi, the Goldsmith, exiled from home by a venal and unjust sentence, such as are usual on the banks of the Arno.* Come, Astorre, let us go to the bridge!''

Astorre did not refuse, since he might well feel the need of breaking the ban of confinement to the purlieus of the palace, which he had not left since stripping himself of the cowl.

'' Have you put money in your purse, monastic friend? '' queried Ascanio. '' Your vow of poverty no longer holds and the Florentine will overcharge you.'' The young men were then crossing the interior hall on the ground floor, at one side of which the counting room was situated, and Ascanio knocked on the little sliding window. A shrewd face appeared, every wrinkle a fraud, and the financial agent of the Vicedominis — a Genoese, if I am rightly informed — handed over to his master, with fawning bow, a purse filled with gold bezants. Then the monk was enveloped by a servant in the comfortable hooded summer cloak of Padua.

On the street Astorre drew the hood far down over his face, more from force of habit than as a protection against the burning rays of the sun, and turned with friendliness toward his companion. '' I say, Ascanio,'' he remarked, '' this errand I had better attend to alone. Do you not think so? To buy a simple gold ring is not too high a task for my monk's understanding? This at least you will believe me capable of? Good-by until vespers, when I shall see you at my wedding!" Ascanio turned away, calling back over his shoulder, "One ring, not two! Diana will give you yours. Mark that, Astorre!" It was just one of those iridescent soap-bubbles, of which the merry lips daily blew more than one and set it afloat in the air.

If you ask me, my lords and ladies, why the monk dismissed his friend, my answer is, he wished undisturbed to enjoy to the last echo the tone of heavenly music which the young martyr to filial love had caused to vibrate in his soul.

Astorre had reached the bridge which, in spite of the torrid sun, was crowded to the edge and bore on its short span a double throng of people proceeding from either shore to the Florentine's shop. Beneath his cloak the monk remained unrecognized, although now and then an inquisitive eye scrutinized the uncovered portion of his face. Nobles and citizens alike elbowed their way forward. Highborn ladies descended from their litters and submitted to crowding and jostling in order to purchase a pair of bracelets or a coronet of the latest design. On all the public squares the Florentine had made announcement by means of the crier and his bell that on this day he should shut up shop after the Angelus. He had no thought of doing so; but what does a lie cost a Florentine!

Finally the monk, hemmed in by the crowd, stood before the booth. The trader, assailed on all sides and turning ten ways at once, merely glanced at him out of the corner of his experienced eye and immediately perceived that he had to do with a novice. "What may I humbly offer to your lordship's refined taste?" he asked. "Give me a plain gold ring," answered the monk. The merchant reached for a goblet on which, after the Florentine style, some wanton scene was depicted in high relief. He shook the goblet, the bowl of which contained a hundred rings in a confused mass, and held it out to Astorre.

Astorre found himself in painful embarrassment. He
did not know the size of the finger that he was to adorn,
and picking up several rings, he visibly hesitated between
a rather large and a rather small one. The Florentine
could not let pass the opportunity for ridicule — we hear
the chuckle of veiled derision in every speech uttered on
the banks of the Arno. " Does my lord not know the size
of the finger which he surely has pressed from time to
time?" he asked with an innocent expression; but as a
wise man he immediately corrected himself, and in the
Florentine opinion that the suspicion of ignorance was
insulting, that of sin, however, was flattering, he gave
Astorre two rings, a large one and a small one, which he
deftly let slip from the thumb and forefinger of his two
hands into the hands of the monk. " For your lordship's
two ladies," he whispered with a bow.

Before the monk had had time to be indignant at this
loose speech he was violently pushed to one side. It was
the shoulder-piece of a horse's trappings that had scraped
so hard against him that he let the smaller ring fall. At
the same moment the deafening sound of eight trumpets
blared in his ear. The military band of the Governor's
German body-guard was riding over the bridge in two files
each of four horses, scattering the throng of people and
forcing them against the stone parapets.

As soon as the trumpeters had crossed the bridge the
monk, hastily concealing in his cloak the larger ring to
which he had clung, rushed after the smaller, which had
rolled away from him under the horses' hoofs.

The old wooden pavement of the bridge had been worn
away by travel and hollowed out in the middle, so that
the ring rolled down one side and was carried by its own
momentum up the other. Here a young lady's-maid named
Isotta, or Sotte, as they abbreviate the name in Padua, had
snatched up the rolling, glistening object, at the risk of
being trampled to death by the horses. "A lucky ring!"
cried the foolish creature exultantly and with childish glee

put the acquisition on the tapering finger of the young mistress whom she was accompanying — on the third finger of the left hand, which because of its delicate formation seemed to her especially worthy and qualified for the narrow band. In Padua, however, as also here in Verona, if I am rightly informed, it is the wedding ring that is worn on the left hand.

The lady showed some resentment at the practical joke which her maid had presumed to play, but was nevertheless herself somewhat amused by it. She exerted herself to remove the ring which belonged to another and yet fit her finger as if made to order. Then without warning the monk stood before her and lifted his arms in joyful amazement. What he actually did, though, was to extend his open right hand, holding his left on a level with his heart; for notwithstanding she had blossomed into young womanhood, he had recognized by the exceptionally slender neck and still more, no doubt, because of the thrill in his own bosom, the girl whose sweet head he had seen lying on the block.

While the dumbfounded maiden cast inquiring glances at the monk and kept twirling the recalcitrant ring, Astorre hesitated to ask it back from her. But he had to do so. He opened his mouth to speak. "Lady," he began — and felt himself enclasped by two strong mailed arms, which took complete possession of him and lifted him from the ground. At the same moment he saw himself seated, by the help of another mailed warrior, astride a prancing steed. "Let us see," some one called out with a good-natured laugh, " whether you have forgotten how to ride! " It was Germano, riding at the head of the German cohort under his command, which the Governor had ordered out for inspection on a plain not far from Padua. Unexpectedly catching sight of his friend and brother-in-law out of doors, he had allowed himself the innocent sport of hoisting the monk to a horse beside him, from which, at a given signal, a young Suabian had dismounted. The spirited animal,

noticing that it had a different rider, gave a few wild leaps.
There was a surging mass of cavalry on the narrow bridge,
and Astorre, whose hood had fallen back and who could
only with difficulty keep his feet in the stirrups, was recognized by the people who gave way in horror before him.
"The monk! the monk!" they cried, pointing at him from
all directions; but the tumultuous squadron had already
crossed the bridge and was disappearing around a street
corner.   The Florentine, still unpaid for his rings, ran
after the troop, but scarcely more than twenty paces; for
he grew anxious for his wares, left to the poor protection
of a stripling; moreover, the cries of the crowd assured
him that he had to do with a well-known personality whom
he could easily find.   He had Astorre's palace pointed out
to him and presented himself there on that day, the day
after, and the day after that.   On the first two occasions
he accomplished nothing, since everything was at sixes and
sevens in the monk's dwelling; the third time he found the
tyrant's seal affixed to the locked door.   The coward preferred to have no dealings with him; and so he lost his
money.

The women, however — Antiope and the flippant maid
had been rejoined by a third, who had been separated from
them by the tumult on the bridge — walked in the opposite
direction.   This third person was a strange looking, as it
seemed, prematurely old woman, with deep wrinkles and
unkempt gray hair, whose expressions betrayed an agitated
mind, and who dragged her neglected but costly robes
through the dust of the streets.

With stupid self-satisfaction Sotte was just relating to
the old lady, evidently her mistress's mother, the occurrence on the bridge: Astorre — for she too had divined
who he was from the outcries of the people — Astorre the
monk who, as everybody knew, was obliged to take a wife,
had furtively rolled a gold ring over to Antiope, and when
she — Sotte — seeing in this the hand of Providence and
understanding the monk's stratagem, had put the ring on

the finger of the dear young lady, Astorre himself had stepped up to her; and when Antiope modestly sought to return the ring to him, he put his left hand tenderly on his heart, thus — she imitated the action — but extended his right hand deprecatingly, with a gesture which throughout Italy could say and mean nothing else than, " Keep it, sweetheart! "

Finally the astounded Antiope put in a word and entreated her mother to pay no attention to Isotta's silly chatter, but in vain. Lady Olympia lifted up her hands to heaven, and on the public highway gave fervent thanks to St. Anthony that beyond all hope and expectation he had heard her daily prayer and had granted her treasure a virtuous husband of her own rank, one of his own sons. Withal she gesticulated so fantastically that the passers-by laughingly put their forefingers to their foreheads. In bewilderment Antiope took all conceivable pains to disabuse her mother's mind of this dazzling fiction; but she would not listen and passionately continued building her castle in the air.

So the ladies reached the Canossa palace and met at the portal a major-domo in stiff array, followed by six extravagantly uniformed servants. Herr Burkhard, obsequiously retiring, allowed Lady Olympia to precede him up the stairway. Then, having reached a desolate drawing-room, he made three graduated bows, each nearer and more profound than the one before, and announced slowly and solemnly, " Your ladyships, I am sent by Astorre Vice-domini humbly to invite you to his esbousal this day " — he painfully swallowed the complementary " ten days hence " — " at the hour of vespers.

Dante ceased speaking. The plot of his story lay spread out in all its fulness before him, but his exacting mind was selecting and simplifying. Then Cangrande spoke.

" My Dante," he began, " I am surprised with what harsh and caustic traits you have sketched your Florentine! Your Niccolò Lippo dei Lippi is banished in consequence of a venal and unjust sentence. He himself is, however, an extortioner, a flatterer, liar, mocker, a loose talker, and a coward — all ' after the manner of the Florentines.' And that is but a tiny flame from the volcano of imprecations which you pour out upon your Florence, a mere dripping dreg from those tercets overflowing with gall and bitterness which in your Comedy you give your native city to drink. Let me tell you, it is ignoble to vilify one's cradle, to put one's mother to shame! It does not become you. Believe me, it makes a bad impression.

" My Dante, I will tell you of a puppet show that, lately roaming about in disguise among the people, I witnessed in our arena. You turn up your nose at my vulgar taste for liking to amuse myself in leisure moments with puppets and jesters. Accompany me nevertheless to the standing room in front of the little stage. What do you see there? Husband and wife are quarreling. He beats her and she cries. A neighbor puts his head in through the crack in the door, exhorts, chides, takes a hand. But see, the brave woman rises up against the intruder and takes her husband's part. ' When it suits my fancy to be beaten! ' she screams.

" Similarly, my Dante, a high-minded man speaks when his native city ill-treats him: ' It is my will to receive this blow.' "

Many young and sharp eyes were fastened upon the Florentine. He silently veiled his head. What passed through his mind no one knows. When he raised his head again his brow was more troubled, his mouth more bitter, and the point of his nose sharper.

Dante listened. The wind whistled about the corners of the palace and blew open a half-fastened shutter. Monte Baldo had sent his first storm of winter. They saw the snow-flakes flying and whirling in the light of the fire on the hearth. The poet watched the snow-storm, and his days, which he felt to be slipping away from him, appeared

to him in the guise of this pale scurry and flight through
a wavering glow. He shivered with cold.

And his delicate auditors shared his feeling. They realized that no home of his own, but only the uncertain favor
of changing patrons gave him a roof and protection from
the winter which covered highway and byway with snow.
All were aware — and Cangrande, who was magnanimous
by nature, was the first to be aware, of the fact that there
beside them sat a wanderer upon the face of the earth.

The prince arose, shaking the jester like a feather from
off his robe, stepped up to the exile, took him by the hand,
and led him to his own place next to the fire. "It belongs
to you," he said, and Dante did not contradict him. On
his part, Cangrande occupied the vacated stool. Sitting
there, he could comfortably gaze at the two ladies between
whom sat the traveler through hell, who now, in the full
glare of the blazing fire, continued his narrative as follows.

While the smaller bells of Padua were ringing for
vespers, there gathered under the cedar-beamed ceiling of
the great hall of the Vicedominis what was left of the twelve
first families, awaiting the entrance of the head of the
house. Diana stood apart with her father and her brother.
There was a hum of low conversation on all sides. The
men earnestly and thoroughly discussed the political aspect
of the union of two of the great families of the city. The
youths jested under their breath at the marriage of a
monk. The women shuddered, in spite of the papal brief,
at the sacrilege, which only those surrounded by budding
daughters saw in a milder light, excused because of the
force of circumstances, or explained as proceeding from
the monk's goodness of heart. The maidens were all
expectation.

The presence of Olympia Canossa caused surprise and
uneasiness; for she was arrayed in conspicuous, all but
royal state, as though a chief part were hers in the approaching ceremony, and she was talking with eery volubility and

urgency to Antiope, who with an anxious heart, whispering and beseeching, endeavored to quiet her excited mother. Lady Olympia had been mightily enraged even on the stairway, where — Herr Burkhard was just then engaged with the reception of two other dignitaries — she had been bidden respectful welcome by Gocciola, who held in his hand a new scarlet cap with silver bells. Now, standing in a circle with the others, she wearied or worried her fellow-nobles by her immoderate gesticulations. With winks and shrugs one pointed her out to another. Nobody, if he had been in the monk's place, would have invited her, and everybody was prepared to see her play one of her pranks upon her host.

Burcardo announced the master of the house. Astorre had escaped from the Germans, had hastened back to the bridge, without finding there either the ring or the ladies, and reproaching himself — although at the bottom only chance was to blame — he had, in the hour remaining to him before vespers, formed the resolution to act, in the future, ever according to the rules of expediency. With this determination he entered the hall and stepped into the midst of the gathering. The impress of the attention directed upon him and the forms and requirements of social intercourse which, so to speak, were palpable in the very air, made him feel that he must not utter the reality of things, electric and sometimes hateful as it is, but must give reality a softened and pleasing form. Thus he kept involuntarily midway between truth and fair semblance and spoke irreproachably.

" Ladies and peers,'' he began, '' death has reaped a rich harvest among us Vicedominis. As I stand clad in black before you, I wear mourning for my father, three brothers, and three nephews. That I, released by the church, believed, after careful consideration '' — here his voice did not ring quite clear — '' and conscientious scrutiny before God that I had not the right to leave unfulfilled my dying father's wish to live on in son and grandson,— this you will judge differently, approving or blaming according to your native disposition for justice or mercy. But in one matter you will all agree: that it would not have been becoming in a man with my antecedents to hesitate and select, and that under these circumstances only the taking of that which was nearest to hand and unsought could be pleasing to God. Who, however, was nearer to me than the virgin widow of my sole remaining brother, united with me as she was by our common inconsolable grief? Accordingly I clasped this hand over the deathbed of a dear one, as I clasp it now "—he stepped up to Diana and led her into the middle of the hall—" and place the wedding ring upon her finger." He did so. The ring fitted. Diana did likewise, slipping a gold ring on the monk's finger. "It was my mother's," she said, "and she was a true and virtuous woman. I give you a ring that has kept faith." A solemn murmur of congratulation from all present concluded the grave ceremony, and old Pizzaguerra, a worthy graybeard—for avarice is a wholesome vice and conduces to longevity—wept the usual tear.

Lady Olympia saw her air-castle burst into flame and burn with falling columns and crashing beams. She took a step-forward, as though to convince her eyes that they saw falsely, then a second step in waxing wildness, and presently she stood close in front of Astorre and Diana, her gray hair on end, while her furious words rushed and tumbled like a city in uproar.

"Scoundrel," she shrieked, "against the ring on this woman's finger cries out another given before now." She dragged Antiope, who in growing anxiety had followed her, beseeching her to desist, out from behind her back and held up the girl's hand. "This ring less than an hour ago at the Florentine's on the bridge you put upon my child's finger!" In such distorted form was the event mirrored in her fantastic mind. "Reprobate! Adulterous monk! Does not the earth open up to swallow you? Hang the brother door-keeper who snored in his drunken stupor and permitted you to escape from your cell! You sought to satisfy your lusts; but you might have selected another victim than a wrongfully persecuted, desperate widow and a defenseless orphan!"

The marble pavement did not open up, and in the eyes of the assemblage the unhappy woman, who thought she had given poor and feeble words to a mother's righteous wrath, read the answer of undisguised contempt, or of a different kind of pity from that which she had hoped to find. She heard behind her back the clearly whispered word, "Maniac!" and her wrath changed to insane laughter. "Why, just look at the fool," she bawled derisively, "who could make so stupid a choice between these two! You shall be my judges, my lords and ladies, and any one who has eyes. Here the darling blossom, the young rose-bud" —the rest I have forgotten; but one thing I know: all the young men in Vicedomini's hall—and more than one among them may have lived loosely—all the young men, the continent and the incontinent, shut their eyes and ears to the revolting acts and words of a mother who trampled upon morality and shame before the child that she had borne, and like a procuress offered to give her away.

Everybody in the hall pitied Antiope. Only Diana, little as she doubted the good faith of the monk, felt, I know not what indefinite anger at the beauty thus impudently exhibited to her bridegroom.

Antiope may have been to blame, because she kept the unholy ring upon her finger. Perhaps she did so in order not to excite her self-deluded mother, thinking that, undeceived by the reality, she would plunge, as was her wont, from haughtiness to humility, and all would pass by with the rolling of her eyes and the muttering of a few words. Or else young Antiope herself had dipped her finger into the bubbling fountain of fairy-land. Was not the meeting on the bridge marvelous, and would the monk's choice of her have been more marvelous than the fate that snatched him from the monastery?

Now she suffered a cruel punishment. So far as the power of an unbridled tongue extends, her own mother had stripped her of every shred of protection.

A deep blush, and another deeper than the first, suffused her brow and neck. Then in the general silence she began to weep loudly and bitterly.

Even the gray-haired Mænad listened with emotion. Thereupon her face twitched with horrible pain and her fury redoubled. "And the other!" she screamed, pointing to Diana, "this hulk of marble, hardly more than rough-hewn! This lumbering giantess that God the Father botched when he was not yet a master and was learning to model. Fie on the clumsy body without life or soul! Who should have given her a soul anyway? Her bastard mother, stupid Orsola? Or the dried-up niggard over there? Only reluctantly did he allot to her the mere pittance of a soul!"

Old Pizzaguerra remained undisturbed. With the perspicacity of the miserly he did not forget whom he had before him. But his daughter Diana forgot it. Incensed and outraged at the brutal vituperation of her body and soul, she contracted her brows and clenched her fists. She became quite beside herself when the lunatic dragged her parents into her invective, insulted her mother in the grave and held her father up to public scorn. A paroxysm of anger seized and overwhelmed her.

"You bitch!" she cried and struck a blow—in the face of Antiope; for the desperate and courageous girl had thrown herself in front of her mother. Antiope uttered a cry that vibrated through the hall and in every heart.

Now the wheel made a complete turn in the lunatic's mind. The utmost fury was swallowed up in unspeakable grief. "They have struck my child!" she groaned; she sank upon her knees and sobbed, "Is there no longer a God in heaven?"

By this time the measure was full. It would have been full to running over before this, but destiny strode faster than my lips could relate — so fast that neither the monk nor Germano, who stood nearby, could seize and hold Diana's uplifted arm. Ascanio grasped the mad-woman about the waist, another youth took her by the feet, and with scarcely any resistance she was carried out, placed in her litter, and taken home.

Diana and Antiope still stood face to face, each one paler than the other, Diana rueful and grief-stricken after the quick abatement of her outburst of wrath, Antiope struggling for speech; she could not even stammer — she moved her lips without uttering a sound.

If the monk now took Antiope's hand, in order to escort away the girl whom his betrothed had maltreated, he did no more than fulfil the duty of chivalry and hospitality. All thought this a matter of course. Especially must Diana have desired to lose sight of the victim of her violence. She too then departed with her father and her brother. The assembled guests, however, found that the most delicate course for them was likewise to disappear, even to the last man.

There was a jingle of bells under the buffet set with *amarelle* and Cyprian wine. A fool's cap came to view, and Gocciola crept on all fours out of his greedy hiding place. According to his way of looking at things, everything had gone delightfully; for he now had unhampered freedom to munch *amarelle* and drain one glass after another. So he amused himself, until he heard footsteps approaching. He was about to slip away; but casting a peevish glance at the intruder, he judged that no flight was necessary. It was the monk returning; and the monk was as jubilant and intoxicated as he; for the monk —

"Was in love with Antiope," the prince's friend interrupted the narrator, laughing convulsively.

"You have said it, my lady, he was in love with Antiope," Dante repeated in a tragic tone.

"Of course!" "How could it be otherwise?" "It

had to come to this!'' ''That is the way it usually goes!''
resounded in the narrator's ears from the entire circle of
listeners.

''Gently, young men,'' Dante admonished. ''No, that is
not the way it usually goes. Do you think a love with
unlimited devotion of body and soul is an every-day occurrence? And do you even believe that you have loved, or
now love, with such devotion? Be undeceived! Every
man speaks of ghosts, but few men have seen them. I will
procure you an unchallengeable witness. There is lying
about the house a book of fairy tales in the mode of the day.
Cautiously turning its leaves, I found in the midst of much
rubbish one true word. ''Love,'' it says in one place, '' is
rare, and for the most part comes to a bad end.'' Dante
had said this seriously. Then he made mock of them, saying, '' Inasmuch as you are all so learned and expert in
love, and, besides, it does not become me to put into my
toothless mouth the words of a youth overpowered by passion, I will pass over the self-betraying soliloquy of the
returning Astorre, and briefly say that when the sensible
Ascanio heard his raving, he was terrified and exhorted
him to reason.''

'' Do you mean so pitiably to mutilate your touching
story, my Dante?'' protested the susceptible friend of the
prince, turning supplicating hands toward the Florentine.
'' Let the monk speak, so that with sympathy we may learn
how he turned away from a rude to a tender woman, from
a cold woman to a woman of feeling, from a stony to a beating heart — ''

'' Yes, Florentine,'' interrupted the princess in deep
emotion and with purple glowing cheeks, '' let your monk
speak, so that we may hear and marvel how it could happen
that Astorre, however inexperienced and gullible, betrayed
a noble woman for a vixen. Have you not perceived,
Dante, that Antiope is a vixen? You have little knowledge
of women! In truth I tell you '' — she raised her powerful
arm and clenched her fist — '' I too should have struck, not

the poor fool, but wittingly the schemer, who at any cost would stand in the sight of the monk!'' And she struck a blow in the air. The other woman trembled a little.

Cangrande, who had not taken his eye from the two women opposite whom he now sat, admired the princess and rejoiced in her strength of passion. At this moment he found her incomparably more beautiful than the delicate and smaller rival against whom he had pitted her; for the height and depth of emotion attain to expression only in a strong body and a strong soul.

Dante, for his part, smiled for the first and only time this evening, when he saw the two ladies so insistently weighing themselves in the balance of his story. He even went so far as to tease them a little. '' What do your ladyships ask of me?'' he said. '' Talking to one's self is unreasonable. Did ever a wise man talk to himself?''

Now a playful curly head emerged from the shadow and a page, who may have been crouching in cosy concealment behind a chair or some lady's train, confidently cried out, '' Great master, how little you know yourself, or pretend to know yourself! Learn, Dante, that nobody talks more glibly to himself than you do — to such a degree that you not only fail to notice us foolish fellows, but even let beauty pass close by you without paying it any homage.''

'' Really?'' said Dante. '' Where was that? Where and when did it happen?''

'' Why, yesterday on the bridge over the Adige,'' smiled the boy. '' You were leaning on the parapet. Then the charming Lucretia Nani passed by, brushing against your robe. We boys followed her admiringly, and from the opposite direction came two fiery warriors, trying to catch a glance from her mild eyes. But she sought your eyes; for not every man has come back with a whole skin after a walk through hell! You, master, were intent upon a rolling wave in the middle of the Adige and were murmuring something.''

" I was sending a greeting to the sea. The wave was more beautiful than the maiden. But let us come back to the two fools! Listen, they are talking together! And by all the muses, let no one again interrupt me, else midnight will find us still telling tales around the fire."

When the monk, after conducting Antiope home, again entered his hall — but I forgot to say that he did not meet Ascanio, although Ascanio with the litter and Lady Olympia had gone the same way as he. For the nephew, after giving over the woman in a state of complete collapse to the care of her servants, had immediately hastened to his uncle the tyrant, in order to serve him with this madcap morsel while it was still hot. He would rather convey to Ezzelino a bit of city gossip than news of a conspiracy.

I know not whether the monk was as comely as Ascanio the mocker had called him. But I see him striding like the handsomest of youths. With winged feet he traverses the hall, as if borne by Zephyrus or led by Iris. His eyes gleam with brightness and he is murmuring sounds that belong to the language of the blessed. Gocciola, who had imbibed a good deal of Cyprian wine, felt likewise filled with a new courage and renewed youth. Under the soles of his feet, too, the marble floor dissolved into snow-white clouds. He felt an unquenchable desire to hear the murmur on Astorre's rosy lips, as one bends over a bubbling spring to listen, and he began to go back and forth the length of the hall beside him, striding and hopping in turn, his fool's sceptre under his arm.

" The tender head that offered itself for the father has now offered and given itself for the mother!" Astorre murmured. " The modest girl, how she blushed! Maltreated, how she suffered! When struck, how she shrieked! Has the image of that head ever left me since I saw it lying on the block? It was ever in my thoughts, accompanied me whithersoever I went, hovered in my prayer, illumined my cell, lay upon my pillow! Did not the lovely head with the slender white neck lie beside St. Paul's —''

'' St. Paul's?'' chuckled the simpleton.

'' St. Paul's on our altar piece —''

'' With the curly black hair and the ruddy neck on the broad block, with the headsman's ax above it?'' Gocciola sometimes performed his devotions in the church of the Franciscans.

The monk nodded. '' Whenever I gazed at it for a long while the ax began to quiver and I shuddered. Did I not confess it to the prior?''

''And what did the prior say?'' interrogated Gocciola.

'' ' My son,' said he, ' what you saw was a child in the advance of the heavenly triumphal procession. Fear nothing! No harm will come to the ambrosial neck!' ''

'' But,'' the naughty fool goaded him, '' the child has grown so tall!'' He raised his hand. Then he lowered it and held it just above the floor. ''And your lordship's cowl,'' he grinned, '' lies thus low!''

The monk was beyond the reach of anything common and unclean. Fire as though from heaven had passed from Antiope's hand into his own and began to burn, at first gently, then hotter and more and more fiercely in his veins. '' Glory to God the Father,'' he suddenly shouted in exultation, '' who created man and woman!''

'' Eve?'' asked the fool.

''Antiope!'' answered the monk.

''And the other, the tall woman? What are you going to do with her? Let her go begging?'' Gocciola wiped his eyes.

'' What other?'' asked the monk. '' Is there any other woman than Antiope?''

This was too much even for the fool. In wide-eyed amazement he stared at Astorre; but a strong hand seized him by the collar, dragged him to the door, and put him out into the passage way. The same hand was then laid on Astorre's shoulder.

"Wake up, sleep-walker!" cried Ascanio, returning just in time to hear the last infatuated speech of the monk. He drew the visionary down upon a bench by the window, looked him straight in the eye, and addressed him with the words, "Astorre, you are out of your mind!"

As though blinded, Astorre at first avoided the searching glances, then he met them with his own, still jubilant, but only shyly to drop his eyes again. "Do you wonder?" he said finally.

"No more than at the blazing up of a flame," responded Ascanio. "But since you are not a blind element, but a creature endowed with reason and will, stamp out the flame, else it will consume you and all Padua. Must a worldling preach to you the laws of God and man? You are wed! Thus saith this ring on your finger. If you now break your troth as you have broken your vow, you will commit a breach of morality, duty, honor, and the peace of the city. If you do not quickly and heroically pull the blind god's arrow out of your heart, it will be the murder of you, of Antiope, and of sundry others, whomever it happens to hit. Astorre! Astorre!"

Ascanio's wanton lips were themselves amazed at the grave and earnest words which in the anxiety of his heart he had given them to utter. "Your name, Astorre," he added half in jest, "is a trumpet call to you to battle with yourself!"

Astorre's manhood reasserted itself. "Some one has given me a philter!" he cried. "I am beside myself, I am a madman! Ascanio, I give you authority over me. Bind me!"

"It is to Diana that I will bind you!" said Ascanio. "Follow me, and let us go seek her!"

"Was it not Diana who struck Antiope?" asked the monk.

"You only dreamed that! You have dreamed everything. You were out of your senses! Come, I implore you. I command you to come! I seize you and take you with me!''

If Ascanio's design had been to banish reality, Germano's clanging footsteps in the passage way restored it. With a resolute countenance Diana's brother stepped up to the monk and grasped his hand. ''An interrupted festival, brother!'' he said. '' My sister sends me—that is a lie, she does not send me; for she has shut herself up in her chamber and is wailing there and cursing her quick temper—we are drowning today in women's tears! She loves you; but she cannot bring herself to say so—it is the way of our family; I cannot do it either. She has not doubted you for a single instant. It is a simple matter: you threw away a ring somewhere, if it was yours that the little Canossa girl—what is her name? Oh yes, Antiope—wore on her finger. Her crazy mother found it and wove her fairy tale out of that unsubstantial accident. Antiope is naturally as innocent of all this as a new-born babe—if any one thinks otherwise, he shall hear from me!''

'' Not I,'' cried Astorre. ''Antiope is as pure as heaven! The ring was started rolling by chance!'' and he related the occurrence with rapid words.

'' But neither must you blame my sister for her violent outburst,'' Germano maintained. '' The blood rushed to her head; she did not see who stood before her. She thought to chastise the mad-woman who had insulted her parents, and she struck the sweet innocence. But the latter must be restored to honor and dignity before God and man. Leave that to me, brother-in-law! I am Diana's brother. It is a simple matter.''

'' You speak in a torrent of words and are yet obscure, Germano! What is your plan? How shall you atone to the poor girl?'' asked Ascanio.

'' It is a simple matter,'' Germano repeated. '' I shall offer Antiope Canossa my hand and make her my wife.''

Ascanio clapped his hand to his forehead. This move of

Germano's dumfounded him. But when, with quick presence of mind, he looked at the matter more closely, he found the heroic measure not so bad; nevertheless he cast an anxious glance at the monk. Astorre, again master of himself, kept as still as a mouse and listened attentively. The soldier's sense of honor sounded like a clarion call through the wilderness of his soul.

"Thus I shall kill two birds with one stone, brother," Germano explained. "The maiden will be restored to her rights and honors. I should like to see the man who will whisper a word behind my wife's back! And secondly, I make peace between you two as husband and wife. Diana need no longer be ashamed of herself either in your sight or in her own, and is thoroughly cured of her quick temper. I tell you, she is immune from that all the days of her life."

Astorre pressed his hand. "You are a true fellow!" said he. The will to subdue his heavenly or earthly passion waxed strong in the monk. But this will was not free and this virtue not unselfish; for it clung to a dangerous sophistry: "Not otherwise than as I shall embrace a woman whom I do not love," Astorre consoled himself, "shall Antiope be embraced by a man who takes her out of hand, to make good the wrong another has done her. We all renounce! Self-abnegation and mortification of the flesh in the world as in the monastery!"

"What must be done I will not delay," Germano urged. "Otherwise she will pass a sleepless night." I know not whether he meant Diana or Antiope. "Brother, you accompany me as a witness; I mean to act in accordance with the customary forms of procedure."

"No, no," cried Ascanio in alarm. "Not Astorre! Take me!"

Germano shook his head. "Ascanio, my friend, you are not qualified for this duty. You could not be seriously regarded as a witness in matters of wedlock. Moreover, my brother Astorre will not allow any other than himself to plead my cause. It is in large part his own. Is it not,

Astorre?" The monk nodded. "Then get ready, brother. Make yourself handsome! Put on your golden chain!"

"And," added Ascanio with a forced jest, "when you cross the courtyard, dip your head in the fountain. But are you yourself, Germano, going to wear your coat of mail? So warlike? Is that proper for a suitor?"

"It is long since I doffed my armor, and it becomes me. Why do you survey me from head to foot, Ascanio?"

"I am asking myself what makes this armored warrior so sure that he shall not, scaling-ladder and all, be hurled into the moat?"

"There can be no question of that," said Germano with the utmost composure. "Will a maiden who has been put to shame and beaten in public refuse the proffered hand of a knight? In that case she would be even crazier than her mother. That is as clear as daylight, Ascanio. Come, Astorre."

While Ascanio thus left behind pondered with folded arms this new turn of affairs, doubting whether it was destined to lead to a nursery of hopeful children or to a cemetery, the friends of his youth were taking the short walk to the Canossa palace.

The cloudless day expired in a glow of pure evening gold, and hark! the bells were just ringing the Angelus. The monk repeated to himself the customary prayers, and it so happened that his own monastery, situated on a slight elevation, prolonged the familiar sounds by a few gently plaintive strokes, to which the other bells in the city yielded the reverberating air. Even the monk shared in the universal peace.

Then his glance fell upon the face of his friend and he contemplated the weather-beaten features. They were lighted up and joyful, with a sense of duty fulfilled, no doubt, but also with the unconscious or unguarded satisfaction of reaching port in the Islands of the Blest under sail of a chivalrous action impelled by the breath of honor. "Sweet innocence!" sighed the warrior.

With the quickness of fury the monk comprehended that Diana's brother was deceiving himself, if he deemed himself unselfish, that Germano was on the point of falling in love with Antiope, and was his rival. He felt a sharp pang, then another and sharper, so that he would have cried aloud to ease his pain. And now a whole nest of angry vipers wriggled and writhed in his breast. My lords and ladies, God save us all, men and women, from jealousy! It is the most tormenting of afflictions, and whoever is afflicted with it is more wretched than the damned in my vision of hell.

With a drawn face and an oppressed heart the monk followed the confident wooer up the steps of the palace that they had now reached. It was empty and neglected. Lady Olympia had probably locked herself in her own apartment. No servants in sight and all doors wide open! Unannounced they passed, in the gathering twilight, through a series of apartments: they stopped at the threshold of the last chamber, for young Antiope sat there by the window.

The arched opening, ending in a trefoil, was filled with the splendor of evening, which in a half-circle enveloped the charming form from breast to neck. Her disheveled hair resembled a crown of thorns, and the parched lips drank in the effulgent heaven. The stricken maiden lay weary under the weight of the shame she had suffered, her eyelids closed and her arms falling limp by her side; but in the quiet closet of her heart she rejoiced and blessed her disgrace; for this had united her forever with Astorre.

And is not even today the loftiest devotion kindled from the deepest pity, and shall it not be so till the end of time? Who can resist the sight of beauty when it suffers undeservedly? I will not blaspheme and I know the differences, but even the Son of God was stricken, and we kiss his stripes and wounds.

Antiope was not painfully seeking to determine whether or not Astorre loved her. She knew that he did; there was

no doubt about it; she was more firmly persuaded of it than
of the breath in her nostrils and the beating of her heart.
Not a syllable had she exchanged with Astorre from the
first to the last step that they had taken on their way
together. Their hands were not any more firmly clasped
at the last: they grew together without pressure; they
interpenetrated like two light spirit-flames, and yet at the
moment of leave-taking were hardly more to be separated
than a root from the ground.

Antiope was appropriating another's property and com-
mitting theft on Diana almost in innocence; for she no
longer had either a conscience or even consciousness.
Padua, with its towers in plain sight, her mother, the
monk's espousal, Diana, the whole earth — all were blotted
out; nothing remained but the abyss of heaven, and this
was filled with light and love!

Astorre had struggled with himself from the bottom to
the top of the stairway, and thought he had won the victory. "I will make the sacrifice complete," he boasted to
himself, "and stand by Germano in his suit." On the top-
most step he once more appealed to all his saints, in the
first place to St. Francis, the master of self-conquest. He
thrust his hand into his breast and believed that, through
heavenly aid as strong as Hercules, he had strangled the
vipers. But the saint with the five stigmata had turned
away from the unfaithful disciple who had disdained his
cord and his cowl.

Germano, standing beside him, was meanwhile composing
his speech, but could get no farther than the two arguments
that at the very beginning had flashed upon his mind. As
to the rest, he was of good courage — he had often enough
made a speech to his Germans in the thick of the combat —
and he was not afraid of the girl. But the waiting he found
as hard to bear as before the battle. He rattled his sword
against his coat of mail.

Antiope was startled, looked up, arose quickly, and stood
with her back to the window and her face scarcely visible,

opposite the men who in the twilight were bowing before her.

" Be of good cheer, Antiope Canossa," spoke Germano. " I bring to you this man, Astorre Vicedomini, whom they call the monk, the husband of my sister Diana, as a competent witness. Behold, I am come to ask you yourself — fatherless as you are, and your mother being as she is — whether you will be my wife. My sister, in her treatment of you, forgot herself " — he could not bring himself to use a stronger word and thereby compromise Diana, whom he respected — " and I, her brother, am come to repair the injury which my sister has inflicted. Diana with Astorre, you with me, — thus meeting, you women can take each other by the hand."

The sensitive soul of the listening monk was wounded by this blunt equalization of wrong-doing and suffering, of offender and offended — or did an adder rear its head? — " Germano, that is not the way to ask in marriage! " he whispered to the armored warrior.

The suitor heard him, and since Antiope remained as still as a mouse in the gloom, he was disconcerted. He felt that he ought to speak more gently, and he spoke more brusquely. " Fatherless as you are, and your mother being as she is," he repeated, " you need the protection of a man! This day has taught you that, young lady. You will not wish for the second time to be disgraced and struck before all Padua! Give yourself to me as you are, and I will protect you from head to foot! " Germano was thinking of his coat of mail.

Astorre found this wooing revoltingly harsh: Germano, it seemed, treated Antiope as though she were his prisoner of war — or did the serpent hiss? — " That is not the way to ask in marriage, Germano! " he gasped. The latter turned half around. " If you know a better way," he said in an ill humor, " speak for me, brother." And making way, he stepped to one side.

Then Astorre drew near with bended knee and uplifted

hands, bringing the finger-tips together in supplication to the delicate head on the background of pale gold. "Can love find words?" he stammered. Twilight and silence.

Finally Antiope murmured, "For whom do you speak, Astorre?" "For my brother here, Germano," he said with an effort. Whereupon she buried her face in her hands.

Germano's patience was now at an end. "I will speak to her in a language that means something," he blurted out, and "The long and short of it is, Antiope Canossa," he bluntly inquired, "will you be my wife or not?"

Antiope shook her little head softly and gently but, in spite of the gathering dusk, in unmistakable denial.

"My offer is refused," said Germano dryly. "Come, brother!" and he left the room with as firm steps as those with which he had entered it. But the monk did not follow him.

Astorre remained in his supplicating posture. Then, trembling himself, he took Antiope's trembling hands and removed them from her face. Whose lips sought the other's I do not know; for the chamber was now shrouded in darkness.

Moreover, it became so still there that had the lovers' ears not been filled with the pæans of tumultuous joy and the singing of heavenly choirs, they might easily have noticed the murmuring of prayers in an adjoining room. This is how it was: next to Antiope's chamber, down a few steps, was the private chapel, and on the morrow came round for the third time the day on which Count Canossa had met his death. Shortly after midnight mass for the dead was to be celebrated in the presence of the widow and the orphan. The priest had already arrived and was awaiting his acolyte.

No more than the murmuring below them did the pair hear the shuffling slippers of Lady Olympia who came to find her daughter, and now by the frugal light of the lamp in her hands watched the lovers quietly and attentively.

That the most impudent fiction of an unrestrained imagination became fact and truth in this tender embrace before her eyes,— this caused Lady Olympia no wonderment; but, to the credit of the mad-woman be it said, no more did she taste the sweets of revenge. She did not gloat over the bitter sorrow that lay in wait for the impetuous Diana; on the contrary, the simple motherly joy prevailed over every other feeling — the joy of seeing her child esteemed at her true worth, desired in marriage, and loved.

When now, illumined by a bright beam from her lamp, the two looked up in surprise, she asked in a gentle and natural voice, "Astorre Vicedomini, do you love Antiope Canossa?"

" More than all the world, my lady!" answered the monk.

"And will protect her?"

"Against the whole world!" cried Astorre defiantly.

" That is as it should be," she said in an appeasing tone, " but tell me, you are in earnest, are you not? You will not put her away as you put away Diana? You are not beguiling me? You will not make miserable the poor fool, as they call me? You will not let my child be again put to shame? You will not seek any evasions or postponements? You will let our eyes see the truth, and like a faithful Christian and true gentleman you will at once lead Antiope to the altar? You will not need, either, to go far in search of a priest. Do you hear the murmuring? One is kneeling in prayer down there."

And she opened a low door, behind which a few steep steps led down to the domestic sanctuary. Astorre cast a glance thither: beneath the rude vault he saw praying before a small altar in the uncertain light of a candle a barefoot friar who was of about his own age and build and who also wore the cowl and rope-girdle of St. Francis.

I believe it was foreordained by Divine Providence that this Franciscan should be kneeling and praying at this place and precisely at this hour, in order that for the last time Astorre might be deterred and warned. But in his feverish veins the medicine changed to poison. When he saw before him the embodiment of his monastic life, a spirit of criminal recklessness and assurance came over him. " With a single bound I cleared the barrier of my first vow," he laughed, " the bar fell away as I leaped over it — why not leap over the second? My saints have not saved me from sin; perhaps they will save and protect the sinner!" In incipient madness he seized Antiope and rather bore than led her down the steps; Lady Olympia, on the other hand, again distraught after a brief moment of sanity, closed the heavy door behind the monk and her daughter, as if to keep a captive and secure a piece of booty, and peered through the key-hole.

What she saw remains uncertain. According to popular belief Astorre with drawn sword threatened and compelled the friar. That is impossible; for since reaching manhood Astorre had never buckled on a sword. It may be nearer the truth to say that the Franciscan — sad to relate — was a wicked monk, and that perhaps the very purse found its way beneath his cowl that Astorre had taken when he went to buy the wedding ring for Diana.

But that the priest was at first refractory, that the two monks struggled with each other, that the cavernous vault concealed an ugly scene — this and more I can read in the blanched and horrified face of the eavesdropper. Lady Olympia realized that down there an outrage was being perpetrated, that she as the instigator and accomplice exposed herself to the severity of the law and the vengeance of the betrayed bride; and, since this was the anniversary of the execution of the Count, her husband, she believed her own foolish head irrevocably forfeit to the ax. She thought she heard the footsteps of Ezzelino: then she fled, crying, " Help! Murder!"

The tortured woman rushed into the passage way to a window that opened out upon the narrow inner court. " My mule! My litter!" she called down, and laughing at the double order — the mule was for the country, the litter for the city — her servants slowly and at their own sweet will rose from a corner where by the light of a gourd-lantern they had been drinking and playing at dice. An old riding master, who alone remained faithful to the unhappy lady, woefully saddled two mules and led them through the gateway to the open space in front of the palace next to the street: he had before now accompanied Lady Olympia on many an aimless wandering. Cracking jokes, the others followed with the litter.

On the grand staircase the fleeing mad-woman, whose impulse of self-preservation, dominant as this instinct is even in the insane, had caused her to forget her dear child, ran into the anxious Ascanio, who, left without news and impelled by apprehension, had gone forth to make a reconnoissance.

"What has happened, my lady?" he asked hurriedly.

"Misfortune!" she croaked like a raven rising from cover; ran down the stairs, mounted her animal, drove her heel furiously into its flank, and disappeared in the darkness.

Ascanio groped his way through the gloomy apartments until he reached Antiope's chamber, which was lighted by the lamp left there by Lady Olympia. As he surveyed the room, the door of the chapel opened and two splendid apparitions emerged from below. The man of assurance began to tremble. "Astorre, you are united to her in marriage!" The resonant name rumbled in the echoing vault like the blare of the trumpet on that day. "And you wear Diana's ring on your finger!"

Astorre tore it off and flung it with all his might.

Ascanio rushed to the open window through which the ring had flown. "It has slipped into a crevice between two flagstones," said a voice from the street. Ascanio caught sight of turbans and iron helmets. It was a squad of the Governor's troops beginning its nightly rounds.

" One word, Abu Mohammed!" he cried, with quick presence of mind, to a white-bearded old man, who courteously replied, "A wish from you is a command to me!" and with two other Saracens and a German disappeared in the doorway of the palace.

Abu-Mohammed-al-Tabîb not only was responsible for the security of the streets, but also entered the innermost parts of houses to arrest those guilty — or those denominated by the Governor guilty — of high treason. The Emperor Frederick had given him to his son-in-law, the tyrant, in order that he might recruit for Ezzelino a Saracen body-guard; and at the head of the guard he had remained in Padua. Abu Mohammed was an elegant figure and had affable manners. He sympathized with the suffering of the family, a member of which he conducted to prison or to the block, and in his broken Italian consoled the sorrowful relatives with citations from the Arabian poets. Though he may have possessed some surgical knowledge and rules of thumb, I suspect that he owed his nickname of " al Tabîb," that is, the physician, first and foremost to certain medical manners: encouraging gestures, comforting words, such as, for example, " It will not hurt," or " It will soon be over," wherewith the disciples of Galen are accustomed to prelude a painful operation. In short, Abu Mohammed treated the tragic tenderly and was at the time of my story, notwithstanding his stern and bitter office, no hated personality in Padua. Later, when the tyrant took pleasure in torturing human beings — you cannot believe this, Cangrande! — Abu Mohammed left him and returned to his kindly Emperor.

At the threshold of the apartment Abu Mohammed signaled to his three followers to halt. The German, who bore the torch — a defiant-looking fellow — did not wait long. At the hour of vespers on this day he had accompanied Germano to the palace of the Vicedominis, and Germano had laughingly told him, " Leave me now! This is where I am going to betroth my little sister Diana to the monk!"

The German knew his captain's sister and cherished a kind of secret fondness for her on account of her tall figure and her honest eyes. Seeing now the monk, by whose side he had ridden at mid-day, standing hand in hand with a small and dainty woman, who, compared with the ample form of Diana, seemed a mere doll, he scented breach of faith, angrily smote his flaming torch upon the marble floor, and hastened away to report the monk's treachery to Germano.

Ascanio, guessing the German's purpose, asked Abu Mohammed to recall him. But the Saracen refused. " He would not obey," he said softly, " and would cut down two or three of my men. With what other service can I wait upon you, my lord? Shall I arrest these youthful buds of promise? "

"Astorre, they are going to separate us! " shrieked Antiope and sought protection in the arms of the monk. She who had transgressed at the altar had forfeited, along with the innocence of her soul, the courage that was hers by nature. The monk, rather emboldened and inspirited by his guilt, took a step toward the Saracen and ere he was aware snatched his sword from its scabbard. " Be careful, boy! You might cut yourself," the old warrior admonished him good-naturedly.

" Let me tell you, Abu Mohammed," Ascanio explained, " this madman is the playmate of my youth, and was for a long time the monk Astorre, whom you surely have seen upon the streets of Padua. His own father defrauded him of his monastic vow and gave him in marriage to a woman whom he did not love. A few hours ago he exchanged rings with her, and now, as he stands before you, he is the husband of this other woman."

" Fate! " was the Saracen's mild judgment.

" And the deserted bride," continued Ascanio, " is Diana Pizzaguerra, Germano's sister! You know him. He will believe and trust for a long time; but if he sees and comprehends that he is a victim of fraud and deceit, the blood spurts into his eyes and in his fury he will kill."

" So he will," said Abu Mohammed in confirmation of this opinion. " He is a German on his mother's side, and Germans are children of loyalty."

" Give me your advice, Saracen. I know only one expedient, perhaps a rescue. We will take the matter before the Governor. Let Ezzelino pass judgment. In the meantime have your men guard the monk in his own stronghold. I will hasten to my uncle. But do you yourself, Abu Mohammed, take this woman to the Marchioness Cunizza, the Governor's sister, the good and kindly matron who for a few weeks past has been in residence here. Take the fair sinner. I intrust her to your white beard." " You may," Mohammed assured him.

Antiope clung convulsively to the monk and cried, more piteously even than the first time, " They are going to tear me away from you! Leave me not, Astorre! Not an hour! Not an instant! Or I shall die!" The monk raised the sword.

Ascanio, who abhorred all violence, looked inquiringly at the Saracen. The latter contemplated the inseparable lovers with paternal eyes. " Let the shades embrace! " he then said in tender melancholy, perhaps because he was a philosopher and deemed life but a vain appearance, perhaps because he meant to say, " It may be that Ezzelino will condemn them to death tomorrow; do not begrudge the devoted butterflies their hour of life! "

Ascanio did not doubt the reality of things; all the more sensible was he, therefore, of the second meaning of the speech. Not merely as prone to levity, but also as a kindly and humane gentleman he hesitated to tear the lovers asunder.

" Astorre," he asked, " do you know me? "

" You were my friend," answered the monk.

" And still am. You have no truer one."

" Oh, do not separate me from her! " the monk now implored him in appealing tones that Ascanio could not withstand. " Then remain together," he said, " until you shall appear before the tribunal.'' He whispered to Abu Mohammed.

The Saracen stepped up to the monk, gently took the sword away from him, prying one finger after the other from the hilt, and let it glide into the sheath by his side. Then he walked to the window, signaled to his followers, and they took possession of Lady Olympia's litter, which was still standing before the door.

Through a dark narrow street they moved in hasty flight: Antiope in advance, borne by four Saracens, by her side the monk and Ascanio, then the turbaned guards. Abu Mohammed brought up the rear.

The little procession passed a small square and a lighted church. Entering the dark continuation of the street, it collided with another procession moving in the opposite direction and accompanied by a multitude of people. A wordy quarrel ensued. '' Make way for the young bride!'' shouted the multitude. Altar boys brought long candles from the church, shielding with their hands the flickering flames. The yellow gleam revealed a litter tilted to one side and an overturned bier. The '' young bride '' was a favorite little woman of the common people whose body was being borne to the grave. So far as the body was concerned, it was without more ado replaced on the bier. But the assembled people caught sight of the monk clasping Antiope to shield her as she leaped from the litter, and knew that he had this day been married to Diana Pizzaguerra. Abu Mohammed restored order. Without further mishap they reached the palace.

Astorre and Antiope were received by the servants with wonder and amazement. They disappeared in the doorway without having taken leave of Abu Mohammed and Ascanio. Ascanio wrapped himself in his cloak and walked along a few paces with the Saracen whose duty it was to keep watch of the palace and who therefore circled it, counting its windows and gauging the height of its walls.

'' A busy day,'' said Ascanio.

"A blessed night," the Saracen replied, gazing at the star-dotted heaven. The eternal candles, whether they rule over our fate or not, wandered according to their silent laws until a young day, Astorre's and Antiope's last, swung the divine torch in the east.

In a morning hour of this day the tyrant, with his nephew, was looking through a small round-arched window of his citadel down upon the adjacent square, which was filled with an excited multitude, murmuring and roaring like an undulating sea.

The collision of yesterday between the litter and the bier and the ensuing tumult had with the quickness of lightning been reported throughout the city. Waking and sleeping, all minds were occupied exclusively with the monk and his wedding: not only with heaven had the dare-devil broken faith, but also now with the earth; he had betrayed his bride, flung away his ring, and, his passions once aroused, had, in the precipitate changeableness of fury, married another woman, a girl of fifteen years, a very blossom on the tree of life; and from the tattered cowl a ravenous bird of prey had come fluttering forth. But the just tyrant, who was no respecter of persons, had caused the house which harbored the sinful pair to be watched by his Saracens; he would today, soon, this very moment, sit in judgment over the crime of the two aristocrats — for the young sinner Antiope was a Canossa — would see that justice should be done the chaste Diana, and would throw out of the window to the virtuous populace, offended by the evil example of its nobles, the bleeding heads of the two culprits.

The tyrant listened to Ascanio's account of the events of yesterday while he cast an observant glance upon the seething mass below. The falling in love did not affect him; only the rolling of the ring occupied him a moment, as a new form of fate. "I blame you," he said, "for not separating them yesterday. I approve your having them kept under guard. The marriage to Diana is valid according to law. The sacrament constrained by the sword or purchased for money is as void as it can be. The parson who allowed himself to be intimidated or bribed deserves the gallows, and if he is caught, he shall hang. Once more, why did you not step between the irresponsible youth and the child? Why did you not snatch a reeling insensate from the arms of a girl intoxicated with a new rapture? Now they are husband and wife.''

Ascanio, whom sleep had restored to clarity of mind and flippancy, tried to hide a smile. '' Epicurean!'' Ezzelino reproved him. But he said in his ingratiating way, '' The deed is done, dread uncle. If you take the case in hand, everything is saved. Both parties I have summoned before your judgment-seat at the ninth hour.'' A bell-tower opposite struck the hour. '' Let it but be your will, Ezzelino, and your firm and skilful hand will unravel the knot as though it were child's play. Love is prodigal and avarice has no notion of honor. The enamored monk will toss over to the miserable niggard that we all know this worthy Pizza-guerra to be, whatever he demands. Germano, to be sure, will draw his sword; but you will bid him sheath it again. He is under your orders. He will gnash his teeth, but he will obey.''

'' I wonder,'' said Ezzelino, '' whether I do right to put the monk out of reach of my Germano's sword. Is it fitting that Astorre should live? Can he, now that, after casting away his sandals, he has worn down at the heels the shoes of a gentleman which he put on, and now that the *cantus firmus* of the monk pierces our ears in a ribald song? So far as in me lies, I will save his vacillating and worthless life. But I am powerless to ward off his fate. If Astorre is destined to die by the sword of Germano, I can bid Germano lower it, but Astorre will run into it nevertheless. I know how these things come to pass. I have had experience.'' And he fell to brooding.

Ascanio shyly turned his eyes away. He knew a horrible story.

Once upon a time the tyrant had captured a castle and had condemned to death by the sword the rebels who had defended it. The first soldier who happened to be by swung the sword. Then, to receive the death-blow, a handsome boy, whose features attracted the tyrant, knelt before him. Ezzelino thought that in them he recognized his own, and asked the boy about his parentage. He was the son of a woman whom Ezzelino in his youth had sinfully loved. He pardoned the condemned boy. But he, goaded and persecuted by his own curiosity and by the envious taunts of those who had lost their sons or relatives in this massacre, could not rest until he had solved the riddle of his exemption. He is said to have drawn his dagger against his own mother and to have forced the shameful secret from her. The discovery of his illegitimate birth poisoned his young soul. He again conspired against the tyrant, attacked him on the street and was struck down with the same sword by the same soldier, who chanced to be the first who hastened to Ezzelino's aid.

Ezzelino covered his face with his hand and recalled to view the scene of his son's death. Then he slowly raised his head and asked, " But what will become of Diana? "

Ascanio shrugged his shoulders. " Diana was born under an unlucky star. She has lost two husbands, one in the Brenta, the other to a lovelier woman. And besides, she has the niggardly father! She will take the veil. What else could she possibly do? "

From the public square below there now arose a roar of grumblings, reproachings, curses, and threats. " Kill the monk! " a few isolated voices urged; but when these were about to blend in a general clamor the popular wrath was strangely transformed into an amazed and admiring "Ah! How beautiful she is! " The tyrant and Ascanio could observe the scene at ease through their windows: Saracens astride of trim Arabian steeds surrounding Astorre and his young wife mounted on mules. The newly-wedded Lady Vicedomini was veiled. But when the thousand fists of the multitude were clenched to assail the monk her husband, she had passionately thrown herself in front of him. This act of love tore her veil asunder. It was not the charm of her face only, nor the youthfulness of her figure, but the free play of her soul, a feeling that took visible form, the breath of life, which disarmed the crowd and carried it away as yesterday it had carried away the monk, who now as a conquering hero rode on without the slightest fear—for he believed he bore a charmed life—in triumph with his warm-blooded captive.

Ezzelino regarded this victory of beauty almost contemptuously. He turned his eye with interest toward the second group of persons who came out upon the square from another street. Three notables, like Astorre and Antiope attended by a numerous retinue, sought to make their way through the multitude. In the middle a snow-white head: the dignified figure of old Pizzaguerra; on his left Germano. The young man had yesterday stormed in terrible anger when his German trooper had brought him news of Astorre's perfidy, and he had started full tilt for revenge, but had been overtaken by the Saracen, who summoned him, his father, and his sister to the citadel and before the tribunal of the Governor at the first morning hour. This had compelled him to reveal to his sister the monk's outrageous deed, which he would rather have concealed from her until it had been avenged; and he had marveled at her composure. Diana rode at her father's right, the same woman as ever, except that her broad neck was inclined by the weight of one heavy thought farther forward than it had been the day before.

The multitude, which a minute earlier would have acclaimed with sympathetic indignation the offended bride on her way to obtain justice, were now, their eyes still blinded with the dazzling beauty of Antiope and their minds comprehending and condoning the monk's treachery, satisfied to murmur "Poor creature! Always made to suffer for somebody or something!"

Now the five appeared before the tyrant who in a bare room sat upon a chair raised only two steps above the floor. Before him stood plaintiffs and defendants face to face; here the Pizzaguerras, father and son, and somewhat to one side the tall form of Diana, there the monk and Antiope hand in hand — all in attitudes of respect, while Ascanio leaned against the tyrant's lofty chair as though wishing to preserve his impartiality and occupy the middle ground between the playmates of his youth.

" My lords and ladies," Ezzelino began, " I will not treat your case as an affair of state, where breach of faith is treason and treason is a crime against the majesty of the law, but I shall treat it as a disputable family matter. Indeed, the Pizzaguerras, the Vicedominis, the Canossas are of as noble blood as I, with the only difference that our sublime lord, His Imperial Majesty, has made me his Governor in these his lands." Ezzelino inclined his head at the mention of the supreme authority, he could not bare it; for except when he wore the military helmet, he always went about bareheaded, after the manner of the ancients, even in wind and rain. " Thus the twelve patrician houses form one great family, to which I too belong through one of my ancestresses. But how we have shrunken through pitiable blindness and the criminal insurrection of some few among us against the highest temporal office. If you believe as I do, then let us bend all our efforts to save what is yet left. This is what impels me to restrain the Pizzaguerras from taking vengeance on Astorre Vicedomini, although I pronounce it in and of itself a just revenge. If you," he turned to the three Pizzaguerras, " are not in accord with my clemency, hear and ponder one thing: I, Ezzelino da Romano, was the first, and am therefore the chief wrong-doer. Had I not on a certain day and at a certain hour let my horse gallop along the banks of the Brenta, Diana would have been married as befits her rank and this man here would still be conning his breviary.

Had I not ordered out my Germans for inspection on a certain day and at a certain hour, my Germano would not have inopportunely set the monk astride a horse, and he, the monk, would have drawn from the finger of the lady whom he now holds by the hand the bridal ring that his evil angel — ''

'' My good angel,'' exulted the monk.

'' — that his angel rolled over to her. Therefore, my lords and ladies, grant me your help in the unravelment and settlement of this complicated matter; for if you should insist upon severity, I must needs condemn myself, — myself first of all! ''

This unusual speech did not in the least disturb the equanimity of old Pizzaguerra; and when the tyrant addressed him with the words, '' Noble lord, your complaint is now in order,'' he said briefly and curtly, '' Your Magnificence, Astorre Vicedomini betrothed himself publicly and quite according to law and precedent with my daughter Diana. Then, however, although Diana had done him no wrong, he broke his troth. This was without due cause, illegal, sacrilegious. Such a deed is a grave offense and demands, if not blood, which your Magnificence does not wish to see shed, at least a heavy penalty,'' and he made a motion as of a shopkeeper who puts one weight after another in the scales.

'' Diana had done no wrong? '' repeated the tyrant. '' It seems to me that she did wrong. Had she not a maniac before her? And Diana vilifies and strikes. For Diana is quick to wrath and unreasonable when she thinks her rights are not respected.''

To this Diana nodded, saying, '' You speak the truth, Ezzelino.''

'' That is the reason,'' continued the tyrant, '' why Astorre's heart was turned away from her; he saw in her a barbarian.''

'' No, my lord,'' the monk protested, offending anew the woman whom he had betrayed, '' I did not look at Diana, but at the sweet face that received the blow, and my heart and entrails were moved to compassion."

The tyrant shrugged his shoulders. "You see, Pizzaguerra," he smiled, "the monk is like a demure maiden who for the first time has sipped strong wine and demeans herself accordingly. But we are sober old men. Let us see how the matter can be adjusted."

Pizzaguerra replied, "Much, Ezzelino, would I do out of good will toward you; for you have deserved well of Padua. But can outraged family honor be otherwise satisfied than with a drawn sword?" Thus the father of Diana spoke and made with his arm a noble sweep which, however, degenerated into a gesture indistinguishable from an open palm—indeed, perhaps even an extended hand.

"Give, Astorre!" said the Governor in the double sense of 'Give your hand' or 'Give money and merchandise.'

"My lord," said the monk turning now with frankness and dignity to the tyrant, "if you see in me a man without principle, indeed without command over his senses, I shall bear no resentment; for a strong god whom I denied, being unable to apprehend his existence, has avenged himself upon me and overpowered me. At this moment he is still driving me like a hurricane and blowing my mantle about my ears. If I must pay for my happiness—beggarly word! miserable language!—if I must pay for the highest pitch of life with my life, I understand the need and find the price low for the privilege. But if I may live, and live with this woman, my wife, I shall not haggle over the cost." He smiled blissfully. "Take all my goods, Pizzaguerra!"

"My lords and ladies," decreed the tyrant, "I assume the guardianship over this extravagant youth. You and I shall negotiate, Pizzaguerra. You have heard that I have far-reaching authority. What should you say to the Vice-domini mines?"

The honorable graybeard said nothing, but the two eyes

lying close together in his hatchet face gleamed like diamonds.

"Take my pearl fisheries to boot!" cried Astorre; but Ascanio, who came swiftly down the steps, closed his mouth.

"Noble Pizzaguerra," Ezzelino now urged, to test the old man, "take the mines! I know that you hold the honor of your house above rubies and that it is not for sale at any price; but I know also that you are a good Paduan and will do something for the sake of peace within the city."

The old man maintained a stubborn silence.

"Take the mines," repeated Ezzelino, who loved plays upon words, "and let him have his minion!"

"The mines and the fisheries?" asked the old man, as though he were hard of hearing.

"'The mines,' I said, and let that be the end of the matter. They yield many thousands of pounds. If you should demand more, Pizzaguerra, I should have to confess myself in error as to your way of thinking and you would expose yourself to the ugly suspicion of trading with your honor."

Inasmuch as the miser feared the tyrant and could get no more, he swallowed his vexation and offered the monk his dry hand. "Just a word in writing, in case of death or other accident," he said then; and taking a pencil and notebook from his wallet, he drew up with trembling fingers the agreement *coram domino Azzolino* and had the monk sign it. Thereupon he bowed to the Governor and begged to be excused if he, though one of the twelve, should be prevented by the infirmities of age from attending the monk's wedding feast.

Gritting his teeth to suppress his fury Germano had stood beside his father. Now he removed one of his mailed gloves. He would have hurled it into the monk's face had not a commanding gesture from the tyrant bidden him halt.

"My son, will you disturb the public peace?" old Pizzaguerra now also admonished him. "My word duly given includes and guarantees yours as well. Obey, on pain of my curse and your disinheritance!" he threatened.

Germano laughed. "Attend to your own dirty business, father!" he muttered contemptuously. "But you too, Ezzelino, Lord of Padua, are without authority to forbid me. It is a man's right and his private affair. If I refuse obedience to the Emperor or to you, his Governor, behead me; but righteous as you are, you will not prevent me from throttling this monk who has made a fool of my sister and a dupe of me. If perfidy should go unpunished, who would care to live? There is too little room on this earth for both the monk and me. He himself will see that when he recovers his senses."

"Germano," commanded Ezzelino, "I am your superior officer. Tomorrow perhaps the trumpet will sound. You are not your own master; you are subject to the Empire."

Germano made no reply. He buckled on his glove. "In days of yore," he said then, "among the blind heathen there was a divinity to avenge broken faith. That has not been changed, I think, by the ringing of church bells. To that divinity I commend my cause!" Quickly he raised his hand.

"It is well," said Ezzelino with a smile. "This evening the wedding will be celebrated in the Vicedomini palace with a masquerade, in exact accordance with custom. I shall give the festival and I invite you, Germano and Diana. Without armor, Germano! With the short sword!"

"Cruel tyrant," groaned the warrior. "Come, father! How can you wish to prolong the spectacle of our disgrace?" And he dragged the old man away.

"And you, Diana?" asked Ezzelino, seeing that only she and the newly wedded pair remained standing before his throne. "You do not accompany your father and brother?"

"With your permission, my lord," said she, "I have a word to say to Lady Vicedomini." Glancing past the monk, she looked straight at Antiope.

Antiope, whose hand Astorre had not released, had taken a passive but deep-seated interest in the tyrant's adjudication of the case. At one moment the loving wife blushed; at another it was a woman conscious of guilt who lost color when she discovered beneath Ezzelino's smile and under cover of his clemency his real judgment, condemning her. Sometimes she rejoiced like a child escaping punishment; again the first consciousness of being the young wife of his lordship, of being Lady Vicedomini, stirred within her. Now, directly addressed by Diana, she met her with shy and hostile glances.

Diana was not to be disconcerted. "Behold, Antiope," she said. "My finger,"—extending it—"wears your husband's ring. You must not forget that ring. I am no more superstitious than others, but in your place I should feel ill at ease. Gravely have you sinned against me; but I will be kind and charitable. This evening you celebrate your wedding with a masquerade, as is the custom. I shall be present. Come in repentance and humility and take the ring from my finger!"

Antiope uttered a cry of terror and clung to her husband. Then, safe in his arms, she spoke tempestuously, "I am to humiliate myself? What say you, Astorre? My honor is your honor! I am now only yours, your heart-beat, your breath, and your soul. If it be your will and command, then I obey!"

Tenderly quieting his wife, Astorre said to Diana, "She will do it. May you be reconciled by her humility, and mine! Be my guest this evening and let my house continue to enjoy your favor." He turned to Ezzelino, thanked him respectfully for his justice and mercy, bowed, and led his wife away. But on the threshold he turned once more to Diana, with the question, "And in what costume will you appear at our house, that we may know you and do you honor?"

Diana smiled contemptuously. Once more she addressed Antiope. "I shall come in the guise of her whose name I bear and like whom I am, the chaste, the maidenly goddess!'' she said proudly. Then she repeated, ''Antiope, remember: in repentance and humility!''

'' Your intention is honorable, Diana? You have nothing in reserve?'' inquired the tyrant in doubt, now that Diana alone stood before him.

'' Nothing,'' she replied, disdaining every formula of assurance.

''And what is to become of you, Diana?'' he asked.

'' Ezzelino,'' she answered bitterly, '' before this judgment seat of yours my father has bartered away his honor and just retribution for his child in exchange for a few paltry lumps of ore. I am not worthy that the sun should shine upon me. It is for such as I that convents have cells!'' And she left the hall.

'' Most excellent uncle,'' jubilated Ascanio, '' you unite the blissfulest couple in Padua, and out of a dangerous complication of events you make a charming tale with which some day as a venerable graybeard I shall delight my grandchildren, boys and girls clustered about the hearth.''

'' Idyllic nephew!'' was the tyrant's satirical comment. He stepped to the window and looked down upon the square where the multitude still held its ground in feverish curiosity. Ezzelino had given orders that those whom he had summoned to appear before him should be dismissed by a rear door.

'' Paduans!'' he now spoke with a powerful voice; and thousands became silent, as though the square were a desert. '' I have investigated the business. It was complicated and there was guilt on both sides. I forgave the offenders; for I am disposed to mercy in every case in which the majesty of the Empire is not involved. This evening Astorre Vicedomini and Antiope Canossa celebrate their wedding with a masquerade. I, Ezzelino, give the feast and I invite you all. Come and enjoy yourselves; I am the host. Tap-room and street are free for your use. But

let no man enter or molest the Vicedomini palace, or, by
my hand I swear . . . And now let each one quietly return to his home, if you love me."

A vague murmur rose to their ears. It trickled away
and vanished.

"How they do love you!" jested Ascanio.

Dante stopped for breath. Then he concluded in swift
sentences.

After the tyrant had given his judgment he rode out at
midday to one of his fortresses which was building. He
was eager to return betimes to Padua in order to observe
Antiope humbling herself before Diana.

Contrary to his expectation, however, and against his
will he was detained at the castle, which was situated several miles away from the city. Thither a dust-covered
Saracen came galloping after him, to hand him a letter
written by the Emperor's own hand, which demanded an
immediate answer. The matter was of importance. Ezzelino had recently by a night attack surprised an imperial
stronghold in the Ferrara country, in the commandant of
which, a Sicilian, his keen eye seemed to discern a traitor;
he had captured the fortress and had put the suspected
commandant in chains. Now the Hohenstaufen called him
to account for this shrewd but bold invasion of his sphere of
authority. Resting his thoughtful brow in his left hand,
Ezzelino let his right hand glide over the parchment and
his pencil carried him along from the first point in his
exposition to the second, and from the second to a third.
He thoroughly discussed with his illustrious father-in-law
the possibilities and aims of a campaign that was impending or at least mapped out; and so he forgot the hour and
the flight of time. Not until he again mounted his horse
did he perceive from the stars, the course of which he
knew — they were shining in perfect clearness — that he

should hardly reach Padua before midnight. Leaving his retinue far behind, he flew with the speed of a spectre over the nocturnal plain. Yet he chose his way and cautiously circled a shallow ditch that the intrepid rider would on any other day have leaped over for sport: he gave fate no opportunity to endanger his return and cause his steed to fall. Once more in full career he devoured the miles of intervening space; but it seemed as though the lights of Padua would never appear.

There, in front of the broad palace of the Vicedominis, which grew dark with the fast-falling night, the drunken populace had assembled. Scenes of unbridled license alternated with harmless merry-makings in the comparatively small square. The throng of people was bubbling over with the spirit of a wild, angry gaiety, a Bacchic frenzy, into which the boisterous students of the university injected an element of mockery and wit.

Presently a drawling ditty could be heard, in the style of a litany such as our country folk are accustomed to sing. It was a troop of peasants from one of the numerous villages possessed by the Vicedominis. These poor people who in their remoteness had heard nothing about the secularization of the monk, but only in dim outlines about the marriage of the heir, had set out before daybreak with the usual wedding gifts, and were just now reaching the goal of their journey after a long pilgrimage in the dust of the highway. They kept close to each other and cowered together, slowly advancing across the surging square; here a curly-headed boy, hardly more than a child, with a golden honeycomb, there a shy, proud lass with a bleating beribboned lamb in her protecting arms. All eagerly desired to see the face of their new master.

Now they gradually disappeared in the vaulted portal where to the right and left lighted torches flared in the iron rings, vying with the last rays of sunlight. At the entrance Ascanio, ordinarily so amiable, was giving directions, as master of ceremonies, in a loud and irritated voice.

From hour to hour the wilfulness of the people mounted
and when finally the aristocratic masqueraders arrived they
were jostled, the torches were snatched from the hands of
their servants and stamped out on the pavements, the
ladies were separated from their escorts and made the
object of lewd jests unavenged by the sword-thrust which
on ordinary evenings would have summarily rebuked such
impudence.

In this manner a tall woman in the costume of a Diana
battled not far from the palace-gate with a circle of clerics
and students of the basest sort which was closing more and
more in upon her. A haggard fellow made a show of his
knowledge of mythology. " You are not Diana," he said
with an amorous drawl, " you are another! I recognize
you. Here is your dove! " And he pointed to the silver
crescent above the forehead of the goddess. She, however,
did not blandish like Aphrodite, but was indignant like
Artemis. "Away, you swine! " she upbraided them. " I
am a chaste goddess and I abhor clerics! " " Goo, goo! "
cooed the beanpole and groped with his bony hands, but
at the instant he uttered a penetrating cry. Whimpering,
the wretch raised his hand and showed his hurt. The hand
was pierced through and through and blood was gushing
over it. The angry maiden had reached behind to her
quiver — the hunting quiver of her brother which she had
appropriated — and with one of the sharp-pointed arrows
had chastised the disgusting hand.

This rapidly enacted scene was already replaced by
another equally horrid, though bloodless. A jumbled music
of all conceivable incongruities and strident discords, resembling a furious quarrel of the damned in hell, made its
way through the deafened and delighted mob. The lowest
and vilest rabble — cut-purses, panders, strumpets, beg-
gars — were blowing, scratching, drumming, whistling,
squeaking, bleating, and grunting before and behind a fantastic couple. A large unkempt woman despoiled of her
quondam beauty walked arm in arm with a besotten monk

in a tattered cowl. This was Brother Serapion who, incited by the example of Astorre, had one night escaped from his cell and for a week had been wallowing in the mire of the street. In front of an illumined bay-window that projected from the dark wall of the palace the horde halted, and with a shrill voice and the motions of a public crier the woman yelled, "Know all men by these presents, ladies and gentlemen! 'Yet but a little while and the monk Astorre shall slumber by the side of his wife Antiope.'" Uncontrollable laughter accompanied this announcement.

Now from the narrow arched window of the oriel Gocciola's jingling fool's cap nodded and a melancholy face showed itself to those in the street.

"Good woman, be still!" the fool complained in a tearful voice that descended to the square. "You hurt my good breeding and offend my modesty."

"Good fool," answered the jade, "be not offended. We but give the name to what the high-born do. We put the labels upon the apothecary's jars!"

"By my deadly sins," gleefully shouted Serapion, "that is what we do! Before midnight my dear brother's wedding shall be loudly proclaimed to the jingle of bells on every square in Padua. Forward, march! Ta-ra-ra!" And he raised his bare leg and sandaled foot through the hanging rags of his dirty cowl.

This clownish performance was madly applauded by the crowd, but the noise of it merely echoed from the steep dark walls of the palace, in which most of the windows and apartments opened upon the inner courts.

In a quiet, secluded chamber Antiope was being dressed and adorned by her maids, Sotte and another, while Astorre at the head of the stairway was receiving the interminable swarm of guests. She peered into her own anxious eyes reflected in a silver mirror which the second maid with expressions of envy held in her impudent bare arms.

" Sotte," whispered the young woman to the servant who was braiding her hair, " you resemble me and have my figure. Change clothes with me, if you love me! Go and take the ring from her finger! In repentance and humility! Bow before the Pizzaguerra girl with folded arms like the meanest slave. Fall upon your knees! Grovel on the ground! Cast all self-respect to the winds! But only get the ring away from her! I will give you a princely reward!" And as she saw that Sotte hesitated, " Take and keep every jewel that I wear!" implored the mistress, and this temptation the vain Sotte could not withstand.

Astorre, who stole a moment from his duty as host to seek out his dearest, found in the apartment two women exchanging their clothes. He guessed what this meant. " No, Antiope!" he commanded. " You must not so evade a duty. We must keep our promise. I require this of your love. I command you to do it!" In the act of transforming this stern decree into a word of endearment by means of a kiss on her beloved neck he was snatched away by Ascanio, who hurriedly represented to him that his peasants wished without delay to present their gifts, in order in the cool of night to start for home. When Antiope turned to reciprocate her husband's kiss, she kissed the empty air.

Now she permitted the dressing to be quickly completed. Even the frivolous Sotte was startled by the pallor of the face in the mirror. There was nothing of life in it except the gleam of dread in the eyes and the glistening of tightly compressed teeth. A red stripe, Diana's blow, became visible on the blanched forehead.

When fully arrayed, Astorre's wife arose with beating heart and throbbing temples, left the security of her chamber, and hastened through the halls in search of Diana. She was driven by the courage of fear. She wished in triumph to fly to her husband with the recovered ring, having spared him the sight of her penance.

Soon she distinguished among the masqueraders the tall goddess of the chase, recognized in this figure her enemy, and trembling and murmuring angry words, she followed Diana, who with deliberate steps passed from the main hall into one of the adjoining rooms which were dimly lighted and only half so high studded. The goddess seemed to exact not public humiliation but heartfelt humility.

In the twilight Antiope now bowed before Diana. " Give me the ring! " she gasped and groped about on the strong finger.

" In humility and repentance? " asked Diana.

" How else, my lady? " raved the hapless victim. " But you are playing with me, monster! You are bending your finger; now you are crooking it! "

Did Antiope imagine this? Did Diana really play with her victim? What a little thing the crooking of a finger is! Cangrande, you have charged me with injustice. I will not undertake to decide.

Suffice to say that Lady Vicedomini raised her lithe form to its full height and meeting with flashing eyes the stern glance of Diana Pizzaguerra cried out, " Girl, will you flaunt a wife? " Then she bent over again and with both hands strove to separate the ring from the finger — a flash, and she was pierced through. Surrendering her left hand, the avenging Diana had with her right withdrawn an arrow from her quiver and had slain Antiope. She sank first upon her left, then upon her right hand, turned half round, and with the arrow in her neck, lay upon her side.

The monk, who after dismissing his rustic guests had come hastening back, longing to see his wife, found her lifeless. With a smothered outcry he cast himself down beside her and drew forth the arrow from her neck. A stream of blood gushed after it. Astorre lost consciousness.

When he awoke from his swoon Germano stood over him

with folded arms. "Are you the murderer?" asked the monk.

"I do not murder women," sadly answered the other. "It is my sister who has sought justice."

Astorre groped for the arrow and found it. On his feet with one bound and brandishing the long missile with the bloody point as though it were a sword, he fell in blind fury upon the playmate of his youth. The warrior quailed slightly before the black-clad pallid spectre with hair on end and the arrow in his hand.

He retreated a step. Drawing the short sword which, unarmored as he was, he carried this evening, and warding off the arrow with it, he said compassionately, "Go back, Astorre, to the monastery that you ought never to have left!"

Then suddenly he was aware of the tyrant who, followed by the whole company that had rushed to the outer door to receive the late comer, stood face to face with him as he entered the room.

Ezzelino extended his right hand, commanding peace, and Germano respectfully lowered his weapon to his superior officer. The raving monk seized this moment when Germano's eyes were upon Ezzelino and drove the arrow into his breast. But he too received a mortal wound from the sword which, quick as lightning, the warrior had again raised.

Germano had succumbed without a sound. The monk, supported by Ascanio, took a few tottering steps toward his wife and, lowered by his friend, lay down by her side and lip to lip.

The wedding guests gathered about the wedded pair. Ezzelino stood in silent contemplation of death. Thereupon he dropped upon one knee and closed the eyes first of Antiope, then of Astorre. In the stillness discordant tones were wafted through an open window. Out of the darkness were heard the words, "Now the monk Astorre slumbers by the side of his wife Antiope." And distant laughter.

Dante arose now. "I have paid for my place by the fireside," said he, "and go to seek the happiness of slumber. The Lord of peace preserve us all!" He turned and strode through the door which the page had opened for him. All eyes followed him as he slowly climbed the torch-lit stairway.